She was tough.

She was a Heller.

She could handle anything.

Certainly taking care of one little baby couldn't be as hard as driving a herd of cattle through a torrential downpour, or smoking nests of snakes out of the barns, or slaughtering cows—or any of the other back-breaking, bone-wrenching work she'd done on this ranch. Could it?

Of course it couldn't. And even if it was, she'd done all that. She could do this. She hoped....

Beth straightened her shoulders and took a deep breath.

But what if, deep down, there was a tiny flicker of relief that her ex-husband had followed her— that her once-beloved Ash had come to Elk Creek— and that she might not be as alone in this as she'd thought?

Beth didn't want to admit it.

Even to herself....

Dear Reader,

Welcome to Silhouette **Special Edition**...welcome to romance. This month's six wonderful books are guaranteed to become some of your all-time favorites!

Our THAT SPECIAL WOMAN! title for March is *The Sultan's Wives* by Tracy Sinclair. An ambitious photojournalist gets herself in a predicament—the middle of a harem—when she goes in search of a hot story in an exotic land. And she finds that only the fascinating and handsome sultan can get her out of it.

This month Andrea Edwards's new series, THIS TIME, FOREVER, returns with another compelling story of predestined love in *A Rose and A Wedding Vow*. And don't miss *Baby My Baby* by Victoria Pade, as she tells the next tale of the Heller clan siblings from her series A RANCHING FAMILY.

Jake's Mountain by Christine Flynn, a spin-off to her last Special Edition title, *When Morning Comes*, rounds out the month, along with Jennifer Mikels's *Sara's Father* and *The Mother of His Child* by Ann Howard White, a new author to Special Edition.

I hope you enjoy these books, and all the stories to come!

Sincerely,

Tara Gavin
Senior Editor

Please address questions and book requests to:
Silhouette Reader Service
U.S.: 3010 Walden Ave., P.O. Box 1325, Buffalo, NY 14269
Canadian: P.O. Box 609, Fort Erie, Ont. L2A 5X3

VICTORIA PADE

BABY MY BABY

Silhouette®

SPECIAL EDITION®

Published by Silhouette Books
America's Publisher of Contemporary Romance

SILHOUETTE BOOKS

ISBN 0-373-09946-0

BABY MY BABY

Books by Victoria Pade

Silhouette Special Edition

Breaking Every Rule #402
Divine Decadence #473
Shades and Shadows #502
Shelter from the Storm #527
Twice Shy #558
Something Special #600
Out on the Limb #629
The Right Time #689
Over Easy #710
Amazing Gracie #752
Hello Again #778
Unmarried with Children #852
*Cowboy's Kin #923
*Baby My Baby #946

*A Ranching Family

VICTORIA PADE

is a bestselling author of both historical and contemporary romance fiction, and the mother of two energetic daughters, Cori and Erin. Although she enjoys her chosen career as a novelist, she occasionally laments that she has never traveled farther from her Colorado home than Disneyland, instead spending all her spare time plugging away at her computer. She takes breaks from writing by indulging in her favorite hobby—eating chocolate.

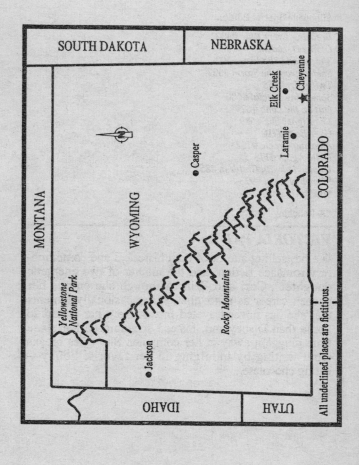

MONTANA

SOUTH DAKOTA

NEBRASKA

Cheyenne

Elk Creek

Laramie

Casper

WYOMING

COLORADO

Rocky Mountains

Yellowstone National Park

Jackson

IDAHO

UTAH

All underlined places are fictitious.

Prologue

Standing at her bedroom window in her family home, Beth Heller looked out over the swimming pool and the reunion that was going on below. Her brother Linc and her old friend Kansas Daye had clearly patched up the differences that had made their private rocky road to love a bumpy ride. Their feelings for each other were so apparent there was almost an aura surrounding them, and seeing it made Beth's heart ache like a bad tooth.

Only one thing could have them coming together so exuberantly—Kansas must have accepted Linc's proposal. No doubt there would be a wedding coming up.

Beth was glad for her brother. She knew how much he cared for Kansas and how worried he'd been that she might turn him down.

It was nice to see that some people did have happy endings.

Even if Beth wasn't one of them.

As she watched, Linc's three-year-old son, Danny, insinuated himself between his father and Kansas, wrapping a possessive arm around each of them.

The little boy's sweetness made Beth smile. It reminded her that her own ending hadn't been completely bad.

One good thing had come out of it.

One very good thing.

With that in mind, she pushed away from the window and went to sit on the bed, pulling the telephone into her lap.

But her hand stalled on the receiver as a terrible temptation washed through her.

What if she didn't tell him?

He might never know if she didn't.

They probably wouldn't see each other again. After all, there wasn't any reason for their paths to cross, since they hardly moved in similar circles. And without anyone in Elk Creek knowing him, chances were no rumors would reach him.

Of course, it was remotely possible Cele would tell him. But Beth doubted it. Technically, as her physician, Cele couldn't divulge confidential information unless Beth gave her permission to, and she didn't think the doctor would break that trust even though she was Ash's friend, too.

But as the temptation grew to keep the information to herself, so did the nudge of her conscience.

"It wouldn't be right," she told herself out loud. Then she added as firmly as if she were ordering someone else to perform a dreaded task, "You have to tell him, so do it and get it over with."

She took a deep breath and forced herself to pick up the phone, punching in the number she'd dialed far too many times lately.

"Just this once, be there," she whispered as she listened to each interminable ring.

"Blackwolf Foundation," the secretary answered.

Beth swallowed hard. "Hi, Miss Lightfeather, this is Beth again," she managed, giving no indication that her insides were tied in knots.

"Hello, Mrs. Blackwolf," came the aloof response, announcing loudly the other woman's feelings that Beth was an interloper.

She considered reminding her former husband's secretary that she'd taken back her maiden name after the divorce, but she didn't. And she didn't bother with amenities, either. It would be a useless effort, she knew from long experience. Instead she plunged in. "I'm still trying to connect with Ash. Is he there now by any chance?"

"No, he isn't. And I'm afraid I haven't given him your messages. He's been even more busy than usual and has had a great deal on his mind."

"Nothing new there," Beth muttered to herself.

If the secretary heard her, she didn't acknowledge it. Instead she went on imperiously. "He's been called away to Alaska to see if the foundation can help in the defense of an Indian boy in trouble up there."

Beth doubted that any phone line in that great snowy north had more icicles forming along it than the one she was on at that moment. But she tried to ignore the arctic chill from the other end. "How long will he be there?"

"He's not coming straight home. He has to go to a seminar he agreed to do at Harvard on Native Americans, after which he's meeting with the head of Indian

Affairs in Washington before he attends a joint tribal conference in South Dakota.''

Old frustrations flooded Beth, leaving her weary and sad and even angry. But she didn't let any of it sound in her voice. "Maybe you should give me some phone numbers where I could try to reach him.''

"Is it an emergency?'' the formidable secretary asked.

"No. But it is very important that I talk to him.''

"It would be best to wait until he gets back here to the reservation.''

Was that a polite way to say she had orders not to give Beth the numbers, or did the protective Miss Lightfeather just not want her to have them? Beth didn't care to push it and discover the worst.

"Yes. I suppose it would be better to wait,'' she said on a sigh, dreading the idea of the delay. Ash might not be home for weeks.

"Was there anything else?'' the secretary asked after a moment.

"No. Thanks anyway.''

Beth hung up, wishing fervently—as she had each time this had happened—that she'd actually reached her ex-husband so she could have told him what she needed to and could finally put this behind her. For that was what she wanted more than anything—not to have to think about it anymore. Not to have to think about Ash anymore, or how he'd react.

Or how she'd bear hearing his voice again...

Then, as if in answer to that, her gaze settled on the desk in the corner of the room, and a new thought occurred to her.

She could write him a letter.

Why hadn't she considered that before? Certainly it seemed like the perfect solution. Getting hold of him was nearly impossible anyway, whether he was on the reservation or not. Writing would give her the relief of knowing she'd gotten it off her chest, and at the same time, she'd have the opportunity to choose her words, to make sure she conveyed just the right tone, just the right message.

Writing would let her keep her distance.

She went to the desk, sat down and took stationery and a pen from the drawer, wondering how exactly to begin.

"Dear Ash," she wrote in an unsteady hand.

Her mouth was dry and she considered going downstairs for something to drink. But she knew she was just procrastinating. And once more the terrible temptation not to tell him at all crossed her mind.

She set her teeth against it and put pen to paper with the determination of the damned.

> I've been trying to reach you since before I left the reservation, but because I haven't had any luck, I thought I'd just drop you a note.
>
> First, it's important for you to understand that I'm not writing because anything needs to change between us. I just thought you should know.
>
> In a few months you're going to be a father...

Chapter One

"He's coming *here? Now?*" Beth said into the telephone to the woman who had been her friend and gynecologist on Wyoming's Wind River Indian Reservation.

"Apparently he arrived home around eleven last night and found your letter in his mail. He was waiting at my office door when I got there this morning," Cele explained. "I tried to convince him to just call you, to talk first, but he wasn't having any of that. He said there were a few things he had to take care of and then he was leaving for Elk Creek."

"You knew about this all day and didn't call me until now?" Beth asked, calculating how long the trip took from the western section of the state to the southeastern corner where Elk Creek was located.

"I'm sorry. I've been trying to find a minute to call you and this is the first one I've had. I don't know when he left, but I know he's gone, because I tried getting hold of him again before calling you and that nasty secretary of his said I was too late.''

Which meant that Asher Blackwolf, ex-husband, could be on the Heller doorstep anytime now.

Lord.

The phone Beth was using was on her nightstand, which was a good thing, because the starch suddenly went out of her knees and she had to sit on the bed. "How did he seem?'' she asked, her tone ominous.

"Surprised—no, make that stunned. Confused—''

"Mad?''

"Maybe. Though it wasn't as if he blew off steam or anything overt. In fact, the way he acted sort of reminded me of you—all bottled up. I can just see the two of you together right now, *both* of you holding everything in, resolving nothing. It's not going to help the situation.''

Beth knew where her friend was headed with this. She'd been pulling for a reconciliation since the pregnancy test turned up positive. "*The situation* will never get better, Cele. The marriage is over,'' she reminded, with an unquestioning finality and a determined straightening of her spine.

"The marriage may be over, but that baby you're carrying means your connection to Ash isn't.''

"Not necessarily.''

"Don't kid yourself, Beth.''

"He has enough other responsibilities already—*more* than enough. Too many. And—''

"Don't kid yourself, Beth,'' the doctor repeated. "This is his child we're talking about—you know—flesh of his flesh, bone of his bone?''

"He didn't want us to have our own children.''

"But now you're going to. And mark my words, babies bring with them big changes."

A click on the line warned that the doctor had another call and Beth was only too happy to end this one.

"Have you seen an obstetrician there yet?" the other woman asked hurriedly.

"Elk Creek only has one doctor and he's not a specialist. But I have an appointment with him in a few days."

"Good. Well, let me know what happens."

Beth assured her friend she would, said goodbye and hung up. But her eyes stayed glued to the phone as her mind spun.

She didn't want big changes in her life. Or at least no change beyond the one she'd just made, moving back to Elk Creek.

She'd come home to the ranch that she, her two brothers and someone named Ally Brooks had inherited to get back in touch with the familiar faces, familiar places of her childhood, to once again be where she belonged.

Because since leaving Elk Creek after high school, she hadn't been anywhere she really fit in.

She'd gone from the laid-back, small Wyoming town where she'd grown up, to six years of college in Boston, with its aloofness and formality. Then she'd joined the Peace Corps and spent four years in Tunisia—a place where men openly showed their affection for one another while women maintained a lower place in society, one far different from the show-'em-you're-as-tough-as-they-are way she'd been raised by her father, the irascible Shag Heller.

Then she'd met Ash. On the plane coming back to the States.

Asher Blackwolf. A full-blooded Native American Sioux.

Until the moment she'd seen him as she'd walked through first-class to coach on that plane, she'd have scoffed at anyone who believed in love at first sight. In eyes meeting and an instant sense of being drawn to a perfect stranger.

But that's what had happened.

And then she'd moved on, feeling absolutely ridiculous.

Until the plane had had to land unexpectedly in Albuquerque because of engine trouble. They'd been stranded there for the entire night.

He'd sought her out at the hotel the airline had put them all up in and asked her to dinner. But when dinner had ended, neither of them had been anxious to say good-night and so they'd drifted outside the restaurant into a balmy New Mexico evening.

Ash had shown her the sights of the old city as if he were a native, had entertained her with Indian folklore and tall tales. He'd talked just enough about himself to intrigue her, and listened to what she had to say about herself with such rapt interest that it had seemed as if they were the only two people in the world. Or at least in the city that slept through the night while Ash and Beth seemed exempt from that need themselves.

And though it seemed hopelessly cliché, there had been magic between them. Along with a sexual attraction so intense, it nearly took her breath away just to remember it....

Not that they'd acted on it until days later.

No, that night they'd merely indulged in the magic. Ash had enchanted her. Plain and simple. If enchantment could ever be plain and simple.

The sun had come up with them still talking and by then it was as if they'd known each other forever. Certainly as if they'd taken longer than that first glance and a dozen hours to fall in love.

But fall in love was what they'd done....

And now, for just a moment, that memory was unbearably sweet to Beth.

A whole lifetime together was what she'd been certain they'd have, for once she knew Ash, she couldn't imagine anything less. Couldn't imagine ever being with anyone else.

And the speed at which it had happened? It hadn't seemed crazy or impetuous or irrational, because being with him had felt so right, so perfect, so destined.... It was honestly as if he were her other half. That single person out there in the world who was meant for her and fate had just wreaked a little engine trouble to bring it to their attention.

She'd married him within the month, without a qualm or a doubt. She'd been so eager to begin her life with him, as if everything that had come before was only a rehearsal and the real thing wouldn't begin until they were wed.

The real thing had meant living on the reservation.

Memories of that were not so sweet.

She'd been accepted there. For the most part, Indian people were a warm, welcoming lot. But there was still a notable group who had resented her being white. Ash's secretary, Miss Lightfeather, among them. And there had been sacred places that were off-limits to her, rites and rituals she wasn't allowed to attend, customs and ceremonies that were very foreign to her.

Not that any of it had really contributed to the breakup of her marriage. Of the three places she'd lived since leaving Elk Creek, the reservation had been the most like home.

No, where she'd really felt the outsider there had been in her husband's life. And that was what had destroyed the marriage.

They'd been divorced for nearly two months now. After wrapping up the details of her job and packing up her portion of the house, she'd driven away from the reservation and back to Elk Creek.

Back home. To her roots, her family, her friends.

"Just stay away," she whispered to the phone, as if the message might reach her former husband.

But he wasn't staying away. He was headed to Elk Creek.

Her brothers didn't know she was pregnant. She'd been putting off telling them, not sure what their reaction would be, and feeling that after herself and her gynecologist, Ash should be the next to know.

But obviously Ash knew now. She had to fill in Linc and Jackson before her ex-husband showed up on the doorstep.

Ignoring the nervousness that had her feeling wound tight as a clock spring, she stood with a new determination. But when she did, she caught sight of herself in the mirror above her dressing table and stalled.

After months of finding her face pale, her blue eyes dull, her usually full lips drawn tight, she saw something different now. And it surprised her.

"Maybe it's that glow of pregnancy finally settling in," she suggested, turning her head just a little, as if a slightly different angle would convince her.

Her dark brown hair *had* seemed fuller lately, she thought. It had been wavier, too, so that the wedgelike cut of it fluffed out at just the right bouncy angle and left the nicest tendrils against her temple. And certainly her sudden surge of energy and vitality had nothing to do with the possible reappearance of her ex-husband.

It was just a normal reaction to her pregnancy.

Her lack of appetite hadn't kept her stomach from beginning to pooch, but it had put a nice indentation in her cheeks that accentuated the high bones above them. And if there was suddenly a hint of pink there? The rosy blush of a healthy mother-to-be. No, the impending arrival of Ash Blackwolf served only to unnerve her.

"So get out of here and do something about it," she ordered.

Taking a deep, steeling breath, she left her room, meeting Linc in the hallway just outside her door as he said his last good-night to his son.

The middle Heller son was a tall, handsome man who'd just agreed to give up his wandering ways and settle down—or what he considered settling down—to open a honky-tonk on the edge of town. He was the less serious of her two brothers, the lighthearted, good-time-Charlie, and he met her with a grin to prove it.

"I need to talk to you and Jackson," Beth said in a hushed voice so as not to disturb her nephew.

"Sounds serious," Linc answered, his tone anything but.

"Downstairs," Beth instructed, leading the way to the wide-open, slate-tiled foyer of the sprawling house that was evidence of Shag Heller's success in both ranching and business. Jackson was standing in the sunken living room near the big-screen television, checking the listings for the evening's programs.

"Beth wants to talk to us," Linc informed their older brother.

Jackson resembled Linc, though he was a shade better looking, just the way he was a shade taller. Both men had the sparkling blue eyes, sharply planed faces, and the dent in their chins that had distinguished their late father.

But appearance was the only similarity between her brothers, for temperamentally, Jackson was more like Shag—serious, down-to-earth, no-nonsense. It wasn't surprising to have him set aside his program guide, turn off the TV, cross his arms over his chest and home in on her with an expression solemn enough for a war summit.

"It's about time," he commented to Linc's announcement. Little got past Jackson, and Beth knew that if either of her brothers had guessed her condition, it would be him.

"I have a problem I need you guys to help me with," she said. "I..." It was harder than she'd thought to say this. But Shag Heller would not tolerate pussyfooting around and she'd learned her lessons from him well. She cleared her throat and blurted, "I'm pregnant."

Linc took his wallet from his back pocket and handed a twenty-dollar bill to Jackson, who accepted it without taking his eyes off Beth for more than a moment.

"Are congratulations in order?" Linc asked, sounding partly as if he were teasing and partly as if he honestly weren't sure the sentiment was appropriate.

Jackson frowned at her. "What I want to know is, who's the father and where the hell is he?"

"That's what I need to talk about. Ash is the father." No money changed hands, this time. Beth was glad to know they hadn't been betting on that subject, at least.

"How'd that happen?" Jackson asked.

Linc threw him a look and shook his head. To Beth he said, "Black-and-white. Everything is black-and-white with him, just like with old Shag." To Jackson, he said, "When hearts and hormones are involved, anything can happen. Anytime. One of these days you're going to run into a filly who'll teach you that."

Jackson just stared darkly at him for a moment before pivoting his gaze to Beth again as if he was still waiting for an answer that made sense.

Beth had no intention of giving one. "The point is, I'm about five months along, but until the day before I left the reservation and finally saw a doctor, I thought stress was causing...my symptoms. So, of course, when I found this out, the divorce was final."

"But the baby's still Ash's," Jackson reminded.

"Well, yes, but that doesn't really make any difference—"

"It sure as hell does." Again this from Jackson.

"Will you let her talk?" Linc asked.

Jackson remained stoic but silent and she went on.

"I couldn't reach Ash to tell him, so I finally sent him a note." Beth drew yet another deep breath, shoring up to hide the uncertainty she really felt about being a single mother. "I explained that this doesn't really have to mean anything to him, that I can afford to support the baby myself and want to raise it on my own, and he doesn't need to be bothered with anything—"

"*Bothered?*" Jackson raised his voice. "It's his baby, not a bother. Is that how he looks at it?"

"No. Well, I don't know. Jackson, will you calm down? Ash didn't want us to have kids of our own for perfectly good reasons I don't have the time to get into right now, and—"

"He doesn't want his own baby? I took him for better than that. I must have been mistaken."

Beth closed her eyes for a moment and then opened them to Linc. "Would you throw some cold water on him so I can get this out?"

"Shut up, Jackson" was Linc's contribution. But it again stalled their brother.

"I don't know what Ash's reaction to the news was. He just got the letter last night and I haven't talked to him. But the thing is, he's on his way here. In fact, he could be here any minute, and I don't want to see him." Again she disguised her own doubts with a mask of strength she didn't honestly feel. "I don't need his help with the baby, and I don't want it. In fact, I don't need or want anyone to give it a second thought. I want you, Linc, to pay attention to your wedding plans and your honky-tonk, and you, Jackson, to just take care of the ranch, and Ash to go back to the reservation and go on about his business just the way he does normally."

"I don't know about that," Linc mused, and Beth knew she'd poured it on a little too thick.

But there was no admitting to anything less than complete independence. Not for her. Not for a Heller. So she forged on insistently.

"Ash and I are *divorced*. It was a clean break and I want it to stay a clean break. This baby doesn't fit in with his plans, anyway, so when he gets here, I want you guys to say I left Elk Creek and you don't know where I am," she finished like a boulder gaining momentum on a roll down a steep hill.

"By God, he owes his own child more than to just turn around and act as if it doesn't exist," Jackson nearly shouted.

"You know, Beth," Linc interjected reasonably. "Jackson isn't all wrong. No matter what Ash's plans were, or how he may or may not feel about it, he has a responsibility to this baby and to you now."

"You don't understand. I don't want—"

The doorbell rang right then to cut off her words.

Beth suddenly felt hot and cold at once, as if something were chasing her, and all she knew was that she had to get away.

"Please," she implored her brothers. "If that's Ash, just tell him I'm gone. Tell him I don't want anything from him but for him to leave me alone."

"Like hell I will!" Jackson headed for the door.

Beth turned a final plea to Linc. "Come on, trust that I know what I'm doing. It's really better if Ash and I don't see each other."

"I don't know about that, Beth," he repeated.

"Look, I'm going to slip out the back door, so telling Ash I'm not here won't even be a lie—for the moment at least. Just do it and get rid of him!" And with that she turned and hurried through the dining room in the direction of the kitchen.

She had every intention of doing just what she'd said, or getting out of the house, into her car and taking off— if not for parts unknown, then at least for the other side of town. For Kansas's house maybe.

But she only got as far as the swinging doors to the kitchen before she stopped.

Go on! she told herself.

And she meant it.

But somehow she was suddenly paralyzed. She turned toward the front door just as Jackson opened it.

And there Ash stood. Tall, proud, almost regal in his bearing and the pure power of his masculinity.

Her heart took a skip she didn't want it to, and then everything seemed to click into slow motion as she watched Jackson double his fist and land a punishing blow to her former husband's jaw.

Ash's head shot to the side, but that was all that was disturbed by the punch that would have knocked any man in Elk Creek across a room.

Then the big, powerful Indian again leveled his coal-colored eyes on her brother and, with a deadly calm, he said in his deep, rich bass voice, "I'm here to see Beth."

The instant the words were spoken, something made him look past her brothers into the dining room, where Beth had stalled. And just the way her gaze had been caught and held by his on that airplane the first time they'd met, so it was now.

Did she heard him whisper her name or only read it on his lips? She didn't know. But she knew he'd said it. And somehow she also knew it was filled with confusion. With pain. Maybe with longing. . . .

No, that couldn't be.

But she suddenly realized those things were alive in her, even if they weren't in him. And she hated herself for it. For the fact that for just one split second it took away the anger she felt at him—for being there, for not having given her the life she'd been so sure they'd have together. Her anger at what would never be . . .

"Go away, Ash," she said in a voice that was barely audible.

In spite of her brothers blocking his path, he took a step forward, as if he wouldn't—or couldn't—stay away from her.

"Linc!" she called, sounding panicky, beseeching her brother for the help she'd requested moments before.

Then she saw Linc's hand go to Ash's broad, hard chest to hold him back.

And that was when she made her escape.
From the man who had fathered her child.
The man she'd divorced.
The man who had, once upon a time, enchanted her.

Chapter Two

Asher Blackwolf stood in front of the mirror in the bathroom of his rented log cabin in Elk Creek's only tourist accommodation—the ten-cabin hunting lodge. With a hand on either side of the old-fashioned pedestal sink, he leaned close and turned his stiff jaw carefully from one side to the other, angling his head slightly to give himself the full view of his jawbone.

There was soreness to go with the slight discoloration where Jackson Heller's fist had landed the night before, but he'd live, he thought wryly.

And a punch in the face was the only thing he'd gotten for his trouble.

"Damn you, Beth," he muttered under his breath, not really blaming Jackson—or Linc, either—for being upset and feeling protective of their sister. In spite of the fact that she wasn't in need of protection.

Even Linc, who he knew to be the more mild mannered of the two, had looked as if he wanted to bruise the other side of Ash's jaw. But then, if he had a sister who was pregnant by her ex-husband and ran out of the house as if she were afraid of him, he doubted that he'd be well-disposed toward that ex-husband himself.

Of course, she didn't have any damn reason to be afraid of him. Or to run from him, for God's sake. And he didn't really understand why she had. Did she hate him that much?

That thought twisted his gut, though he told himself the response was uncalled-for. Whether she loved him or hated him shouldn't matter. Their marriage was over.

But what he had every right to resent was her leaving him alone with his two former brothers-in-law glaring at him as if he were a mass murderer.

For three hours he'd sat there facing them, none of them knowing what to say, none of them happy. Jackson downright mad, and Linc only repeating again and again that Beth had begged him to tell Ash to go back to the reservation and leave her alone, and suggesting that maybe that was what he should do.

Ash had certainly spent more pleasant evenings.

It hadn't even been informative. Beyond the fact that their sister was pregnant, neither Linc nor Jackson knew any more than Ash did.

And he had plenty of questions. Like why the hell she hadn't come to him personally with news like this. Why she'd waited so long. Why she hadn't told him before the divorce was final. What they were going to do now...

Ash let his head hang down between his shoulders as the impact of the news washed over him the way it had been every few minutes since he'd found out.

She was *pregnant*...

Was she happy about it? Unhappy about it? Did she resent that the baby was his? Was that why she wanted to exclude him—so she could try forgetting it was his child at all?

No doubt about it, there were questions he needed answered.

Linc had assured him he'd try to reason with her about seeing him. But whether or not his former brother-in-law convinced her to agree to it, Beth Heller was going to see him today. She could do it willingly, or she could do it unwillingly, but she was going to see him.

Because the one thing he wouldn't do was accept her orders to ignore the bombshell she'd dropped on him.

He pushed off the sink and went back into the room where one double bed, a small table with two chairs and a bureau with a TV on top of it filled the space. His suitcase was open on the rack at the foot of the bed and as he bent over it to get a clean shirt, he caught sight of Beth's letter out of the corner of his eye.

His teeth clenched at just the thought of it, but rather than taking his shirt out the way he'd meant to, his hand reached to the letter.

He'd read it a dozen times since finding it in the mail that had accumulated while he was gone, but for some reason he was compelled to open it and read it yet again.

It was just like her, he thought, feeling a dull ache in his jaw from muscles that tightened in anger.

She didn't want his help.

She didn't need it.

She had everything planned out. Everything under control. Everything taken care of.

He was superfluous.

Excess baggage.

No, she hadn't said he was superfluous or excess baggage. Not in so many words, anyway. But he knew it was what she was telling him.

But, damn it, this baby was his, too. And he wasn't going to be written out of its life before it was even born. Or after, either, for that matter.

He sat on the edge of the bed and stared at the words on the white paper.

In a few months you're going to be a father... Once more that wave of shock and awe and disbelief washed through him.

They were going to have a *baby*.

He and his beautiful Beth...

Ash's eyes pinched closed in rejection of that thought that had come on its own and he shook his head the way a dog shakes off water.

She wasn't *his* Beth anymore.

They were divorced and he had no claim on her.

Or did he? The baby changed things, that was for sure. It tied them together despite the legal severing of their marriage.

But did it give him claim to Beth again?

Probably not.

Not that he wanted claim to her again.

They'd been right to get divorced. Somehow they'd lost that precious spark that had brought them together. She went her way. He went his. And every now and then they met up. Usually accidentally. Or coincidentally.

Or in bed...

But he was better off not thinking about that.

He still held the letter, and once more he focused on the impeccable handwriting on the crisp white stationery, hating the words that were there. Not for their message of the baby, but for what they conveyed about Beth not needing him.

It didn't surprise him. Why should this be any different?

But he couldn't help wishing that just this once it had been.

Deep down, in a secret place he didn't want to acknowledge even to himself, he envisioned the letter he wished he'd received. *We're going to have a baby and I need you by my side. I want you...*

He blew out a wry, mirthless sigh at the very thought.

Not Beth Heller. The earth could open up under her feet and she wouldn't holler for help.

She was the damned most self-sufficient person he knew. And the stubbornest.

Not that anyone would think it to look at her. She was so thin, so fragile looking, with that alabaster skin and those wide blue eyes the color of Colorado columbines. Delicate—that was the word for how she appeared, her high-cheekboned face haloed in that thick, coffee-bean-hued hair, those soft pale lips, that thin nose that could have belonged to a porcelain doll...

Ha! She was no porcelain doll. Beneath it all beat a will and determination stronger than any man's. Furniture to move? Beth Heller would do it herself. Or die trying. A tight lid to open? She'd beat on it, run it under hot water, use pliers, nearly break the jar rather than admit she couldn't do it herself. Heavy boxes? If she couldn't drag them, she'd devise something else—once she'd used roller skates—but she sure as hell wouldn't ask for help.

Funny—when they'd first met, her independence had been one of the things that had attracted him to her. But her determination had somehow lost its charm. Ash wished that, just once, she would break down and admit she needed him.

But maybe what she'd told him was the truth. That even pregnant with his child, she didn't want him or need him.

It had been such a long time since Ash had been able to read her feelings. She'd never been the type to say "I love you." In the early months of their marriage, though, he'd always seemed to sense what she was feeling.

Somewhere, they'd lost their connection. She hadn't so much as let him comfort her in her grief when her father had died. All she'd shown him was a stiff upper lip. Stoicism. Resolution. Death, she'd said to dismiss his concern for how she might be taking the news, was a fact of life.

Then, in the middle of the night when she'd thought he was asleep, she'd locked herself in the bathroom to cry for the old cuss. And when Ash went looking for her, would she unlock the door and let him hold her? Let him console her? Not Beth Heller. She'd gotten angry that he'd discovered her and she refused to open the door. She'd spent the whole damn night in that bathroom. And when she'd come out the next morning? Not a word about it. Not a tear or a sign that she'd ever shed one.

And he'd been left with empty arms aching to hold a woman who didn't want him to.

No, the way she looked was no indication of the way she was. It didn't reflect the core of steel that she wanted everyone to believe ran right through the center of her.

Whether it really did or not.

Ash threw the letter back into his suitcase and snatched his shirt with a vengeance.

That was all old business. Finished. Now there was something else to deal with, something else to concentrate on.

They were going to have a baby.

In spite of it all.

Late June sunshine flooded the cheery guest bedroom in which Beth woke up that morning. All of Kansas Daye's house was like that particular room—bright, warm, homey, comforting. But it didn't help the knots that formed in Beth's stomach the minute her eyes opened and she recalled the reason she'd appeared on her old friend's doorstep the night before, asking to sleep over.

She'd driven around for a long time after leaving the ranch, hoping to give her brothers enough of a chance to get rid of Ash for her.

But when she'd gone back, his car was still there.

She'd been afraid he was stonewalling, refusing to leave until he spoke to her, and so she'd sought refuge with Kansas.

Lord, but she didn't want to confront him!

It had probably been unrealistic, but she really had hoped he would take her letter seriously and leave her alone. That he'd just go on with his life the way it was and let her go on with hers.

But no, he had to come to Elk Creek.

Why, exactly? she wondered, staring up at the ceiling.

There wasn't anything he could do. It wasn't as if he could take a turn carrying this baby. Any involvement on his part couldn't happen until the child was born, and that wouldn't be for months yet. So what was the point?

Maybe he'd come just to let her know how unhappy about it he was.

After all, she knew he'd been against their having kids of their own. On the few occasions when the subject had come up, he'd talked about adopting hard-to-place Indian babies at risk of being given to people outside of their culture when homes with Native American parents couldn't be found.

But he'd only spoken of it as something far down the road, when he wasn't so busy with work, and Beth hadn't believed that it would ever happen, that Ash would ever have time to be a father to any child.

Any more than he'd had the time to be a husband.

The trouble she'd had reaching him to tell him she was pregnant wasn't out of the ordinary. Sometimes she thought he must believe there wasn't another person in the world who could deal with the problems and causes of Native Americans. Maybe it was a cliché, but it was true that the man had been more married to his work than to her.

The Blackwolf Foundation. Demanding wife, exacting mistress and needy child, all rolled into one package.

Ash was head of an organization he'd established with a portion of the substantial estate he'd inherited from his paternal grandfather.

Beth had never met her former husband's namesake. The man had been dead several years when she and Ash first encountered each other, but she knew he'd been a renowned and very successful metal sculptor who had amassed a fortune late in life, a fortune large enough to make Ash a wealthy man and still help fund the foundation.

And the foundation did good work. Valid work. Necessary work in areas of drug and alcohol rehabilitation, in programs that trained Native Americans for better jobs, in family counseling, in aid for the needy, in college grants and scholarships, as well as keeping an eye on legislation that might help or hinder the rights of Indians, and helping to find legal representation for Native American individuals or businesses that ran into problems.

And Ash did it all.

He was a hands-on kind of person. When there was a problem—and there was *always* a problem somewhere—he was right there to see what could be done.

She admired that about him. She respected his devotion to the plights of his people. She was impressed that a person who could easily have used his inheritance to become a man of leisure was instead the first person to roll up his sleeves and dig in.

But it made for a lousy husband.

As the years had passed she'd come to feel almost like an incidental speck in the corner of the much bigger picture of his life.

His secretary had been more involved with him than Beth had. At least the daunting Miss Lightfeather always knew where he was at any given moment and how to reach him. Beth had rarely known even that.

There had been many times in the past when one crisis ran into another commitment that overlapped yet another engagement or responsibility and kept Ash away for so long that she'd begin to wonder if he even remembered he had a wife.

She'd tried hard to keep busy with her own work, but accounting was a nine-to-five job for the most part, and it still left her with long evenings and weekends alone.

She'd volunteered for his pet projects and programs, hoping that immersing herself in his causes, his interests, might bring them together.

He'd appreciated that, welcomed her help and her contribution, but before long he'd start to act as if she were his delegate, leaving her to represent him while he went on to other pressing obligations.

She'd made friends and built a social life, but somehow it wasn't enough. Something was missing from her life.

And then, late one night, she'd realized she was just plain lonely. Deep down, depressingly lonely.

The oddest thing about it was that it had happened after a terrific round of lovemaking.

Not that their lovemaking wasn't always terrific. It was. It was the one thing in their marriage that was an unqualified success. But each encounter in bed only made her hungry for more of him. More time with him. The chance to really get to know him. To talk to him. To have a life together.

But that never happened and for some reason, that night, she'd finally accepted that it never would. That she'd never be first on his list of priorities. And she'd finally admitted to herself that she couldn't accept it any longer.

She'd sat up the rest of the night and when his alarm went off at five the next morning, she'd told him she was divorcing him.

And he hadn't really argued.

Beth swallowed back the lump that memory could still put in her throat.

He'd moved in with his maternal grandfather while Beth filed the necessary papers and finished tax season, wrapping up her job and her life on the reservation at about the same time the final decree was handed down.

Then she'd packed her things. And, for the first time, she'd begun to wonder about some of what was happening to her physically. And what wasn't happening, and hadn't for a long while.

So, just before she was set to leave, she'd gone in to see Cele.

That was when her friend and doctor had told her that missed periods and fatigue were not because of the stress of divorcing a man she would have rather had a future with.

So this is what has to happen to get him to take notice, she thought.

Unfortunately, it was too late.

Too late for anything more than wondering if things would be different had she known on that last night they'd made love that she was already carrying his child.

Beth got out of bed and pulled on the clothes she'd been wearing when she'd arrived. How much easier it would be if she'd divorced Ash because she didn't have any feelings for him anymore. Because she wasn't attracted to him anymore. Because sparks couldn't be ignited between them.

But the fact that she still cared didn't change anything.

She'd learned very well what being married to him was like and there was no going back to it.

Not that Ash would even want her back.

The sound of her brother's voice drifted to Beth even before she reached her friend's kitchen. Linc was teasing Kansas about how deprived he'd felt not seeing her the night before.

When Beth joined them she found Linc sitting on a kitchen chair with Kansas on his lap. The evidence of their playful affection gave her an instant twinge of jealousy that she fought back.

"Morning," she said to announce herself.

"Hi," Kansas responded with a laugh in her voice as Linc nibbled her earlobe. Then she pushed out of his arms and stood.

Beth was grateful for that.

"How about some breakfast?" Kansas offered. "I'll make you pancakes and top them with powdered sugar and a few sprinkles of fresh squeezed orange juice like we used to have after our sleepovers when we were kids."

Beth smiled at the memory. She and Kansas had grown up together, but their friendship had really blossomed when they were teenagers. They'd spent a lot of time together through junior high and high school, then drifted apart when they'd gone off to different colleges and over the years that followed. But it was good to rekindle that friendship now. Especially when Beth really needed a friend.

What she didn't need was food. Her stomach was still in knots. "Let's do our special pancakes another time. I'm not hungry right now."

"Coffee? Tea? Milk?"

"Nothing. Thanks."

Kansas refilled Linc's cup and then sat on a separate chair. Beth took a third, all the while feeling strongly her brother's unwavering stare.

"I think you got things confused last night, Liz-a-Beth," he finally said, using the name he'd teased her with when they were kids, clearly meaning to soften the chastising tone in his voice. "I was supposed to come here to be with Kansas and you should have been the one with Ash."

Beth grimaced. "How did it go?"

"It was no party, I'll tell you that. We didn't know what the hell to say to him and he sat there waiting for you damn near till midnight. I couldn't leave him alone with Jackson and the only way I could get him out of there was to give him my word I'd try convincing you to see him today."

"What about convincing him to go back to the reservation?"

"I let him know that's what you wanted him to do. But he's not budging." Linc frowned at her. "And I can't say as I blame him. In his shoes there's no way I would."

"I thought you were on my side."

"I am, I am," he assured her halfheartedly. "I just don't understand what your side is, exactly."

"What's Ash's side?" she asked rather than explaining herself.

"Well, I don't know that, either. I only know that if my wife were pregnant with my baby and ran out the back door rather than talking to me about it, I'd want to turn her over my knee."

Was he telling her that was what Ash wanted to do? That he was that angry? "I'm not his wife. Not anymore," she said defensively, as if that were an answer that made sense.

"That's just splittin' hairs," Linc said.

"Don't you think you should talk to him, Beth?" Kansas put in quietly, breaking the silence she'd held until then.

"Yes, I know I should," Beth grumbled, more to herself than to either of them.

"*Should* nothing, he isn't going to let you get away with not talking to him," Linc warned her.

Beth rolled her eyes. "I said everything I needed to in the letter I wrote him. I don't know what else he wants to hear."

"Maybe he has something to say to you."

That tightened the knots in her stomach.

Linc went on, "He was going from our place to the hunting lodge to take a cabin there. We could have put him up but—"

"Oh, I'm glad you didn't." Beth breathed out a gust of panicky air at just the thought. Wouldn't *that* have been grand? She could have had Ash in the bedroom right next to hers. She'd have met him coming and going at all hours of the day and night; she'd have had to see him the way he was at home—relaxed, casual, sexy, appealing...

"It was definitely better that you didn't invite him to stay at the ranch," she reiterated firmly, as if it still might be a possibility.

"I felt rude and inhospitable not asking him to, but between you running out and Jackson all het up over this thing, I didn't think I'd better."

"Jackson didn't hit him again, did he?" Beth asked, her concern sounding.

"No. Just the one punch. In fact, he calmed down considerably when he realized it wasn't as if Ash was denying his responsibilities. But still, I didn't think it was a good idea to have Ash close at hand in case he did something else Jackson might take offense to. You know how he is. He always thought he needed to fight your battles for you."

"I hope this won't be a battle."

Linc's expression said he didn't see it being anything but.

It made Beth wonder yet again just how unhappy Ash was about her pregnancy.

But there was no sense sitting around worrying about it. Even if she was susceptible to just the sight of her former husband, Shag had taught her to ignore weaknesses like that. And certainly not to let anyone else see them. Running out the night before had been a show of weakness. It wasn't something she was proud of.

She had to tough this out, she told herself. And that was what she was going to do.

Besides, apparently Ash wasn't leaving, and if she had to deal with him sooner or later, it might as well be sooner.

She laid both of her palms on the tabletop and pushed herself to her feet. "Do me a favor and call him at the lodge, would you? Tell him to come back out to the ranch in an hour. That'll give me a chance to shower and put on clean clothes." And having her brother make the call would buy her that much more time before she had to actually talk to Ash herself.

Linc eyed her suspiciously. "You aren't just stalling so you can go home, pack a bag and leave town, are you?"

Tempting thought. But it would only postpone the inevitable and she knew it. At that moment she was wishing she'd have stayed to confront her former husband the night before. Maybe he'd be on his way back to the reservation by now if she had. "I'll be at the ranch when he gets there," she assured.

Then she thanked Kansas for the refuge and left, trying not to notice that the knots in her stomach had turned to all-out jitters.

An hour didn't give her much time, and once she was back at the ranch, Beth rushed through her shower.

Choosing what to wear took longer. She had a bit of a stomach but not so much that she couldn't still wear some of her regular clothes as long as they were fairly loose fitting.

She didn't want to appear dressed up, but she didn't want to look sloppy, either, so in the end she opted for a tunic T-shirt and a pair of stirrup pants that she thought looked casually chic.

Her hair air-dried and required only some scrunching with her hand to give it bounce. But she was careful about the makeup she applied. A touch of pale eye shadow, just enough mascara to darken her lashes, and a hint of lipstick. She'd have used blush, too, but again this morning her color was naturally high and she didn't need it.

All in all, she was pleased with the results, and though she told herself it shouldn't matter, it did. Regardless of how she felt about this meeting, it was important to her that she seem cool, calm, collected. And if one look at her made Ash think he'd been a fool to take her for granted? Well, great! It wouldn't change anything, but she wouldn't mind at all if he suffered a pang or two of regret.

Feeling more or less on top of things, she headed downstairs.

She'd be fine, she thought, running through a scenario of the meeting in her mind. They'd have a simple conversation. She'd confirm that she'd meant what she'd written in her letter. He'd want to know when the baby was due and make sure she had a plan, that she really was willing to have and raise it on her own. He'd tell her to notify him when it was born. Maybe he'd want to arrange some sort of visitation. Then he'd leave. He'd go back to the reservation. She'd go on the way she'd intended all along, and everything would be fine. Just fine.

So how come at the bottom of the steps she wilted like an unwatered rose?

In the three weeks since she'd realized she was pregnant, she'd thought mostly of Ash. Of trying to get the news to him. Of wondering what his reaction would be. Of convincing him she didn't need or want his help or anything from him.

But now that she was actually faced with sending him away, she suddenly felt herself confronting the fact that she wasn't convinced herself.

Oh, sure, doubts had been creeping across her mind all along and she'd been fighting them. But now they weren't only creeping. They'd walked right in and taken over.

Could she really do it all alone?

Having a child was a daunting prospect. Raising it by herself was an even more daunting one.

She'd be a single mother. On her own no matter what the child needed, no matter when or where.

There wouldn't be anybody else to turn to for relief when she was too tired to move. No one at all to share the load. Or the joy. No one to help make decisions. To worry with. No one but her.

There wouldn't be anyone to let her know if she was doing a good job or a bad one. Or anyone to be a sounding board when she was unsure of herself.

There wouldn't be anyone but her...

"Oh, my God," she whispered. "What am I doing?"

But what was her alternative to being alone in this? she asked herself.

There wasn't one. Because even if she and Ash were still married, she'd be almost as alone with a baby as without one.

Ash didn't love her anymore. His thoughts were elsewhere. If he were to take her back out of a sense of obligation, their second marriage would be as doomed as the first. And their baby would never know a full-time father.

When Beth needed relief from night after night of interrupted sleep, he'd be in Washington lobbying for the return of more Native American lands.

When the baby had colic, he'd be making sure a plumber was doing what needed to be done at the rehab center.

When the baby took its first step, he wouldn't be there to share the moment with her, he'd be off doing paperwork at the office.

When she was up worrying about bad behavior in school, he'd be making plans for fund-raising for new scholarship programs.

No, she was alone in this no matter how she looked at it. At least now, living in Elk Creek, she had her family and friends. She could count on them. She could turn to Linc or Jackson or Kansas when she needed help or moral support or bolstering.

And she wouldn't have to go through Miss Lightfeather to do it.

Not that she expected to need a lot of help, anyway, she thought as she began to make some headway at shoving her doubts back into the corner of her mind.

Her father had taught her to be independent, not to need anything from anyone. In fact, there would have been hell to pay if old Shag were around and knew she'd even had this lapse in confidence. Weak, sniveling, whining—that's what he'd have called it. And he wouldn't have tolerated it. He'd have sent her out to work twice as hard, made her do something so bad that no matter what she was fretting over, it would end up seeming like nothing next to what he'd have her doing.

She was tough.

She was a Heller.

She could handle anything.

She hoped....

Certainly taking care of one little baby couldn't be as hard as driving a herd of cattle through a torrential downpour, or smoking nests of snakes out of the barns, or slaughtering cows, or any of the gazillion other back-breaking, bone-wrenching work she'd done on this ranch.

Could it?

Of course it couldn't. And even if it was, she'd done all that. She could do this.

She hoped....

She straightened her shoulders and took a deep breath.

Now wasn't the time to doubt herself. She had to concentrate on dealing with Ash.

She headed for the living room, meaning to sit quietly, maybe read a magazine until he got there. But somehow her feet took a detour and she ended up across the entranceway at the window beside the door, with one hand nudging the drapery panel aside just enough to peek through.

The house was built in an H-shape and she looked out over a bricked courtyard between the two front arms of the H. Beyond that was the circular driveway that made a horseshoe out of the road that connected them to the highway into town.

Her car was parked at the edge of the courtyard because she'd been in too much of a hurry to pull around to the garages, which were in a separate building just off the south corner of the house.

She considered going out now and moving her car, but just as she was about to, she spotted Ash's black sedan turning onto the road.

Lord, how she hated the fact that that was all it took to kick her heart into double time. Much as she wanted to let go of that curtain rather than watch him coming, she was frozen to the spot.

His windows were tinted, so she couldn't see him until he got out of his car.

And then all she could think was that she wished he'd have stayed away.

The man was striking. All the dignity of his proudest ancestors was there in his straight, broad shoulders. And though he was wearing a pale yellow shirt with the sleeves rolled to his elbows, and a pair of khaki slacks, she knew well what was inside of his clothing—a hard, muscular body that could easily have gone into battle covered with not much more than war paint.

But at that moment there was nothing about him that wasn't the modern man. Even his long black hair tied at his nape could have served a rock singer. He always wore it that way, freeing it only for ceremonial rituals, and he was easily man enough not to be feminized by it even slightly. The faint dusting of premature gray at his temples didn't hurt anything, either. In fact it contributed a dash of maturity that was all the more enticing.

As Beth watched, he went around to the trunk of his car and opened it. But she didn't pay much attention to the small orange crate he took from it. She was more intent in relearning his profile. She'd never seen a man with bones as beautiful—the broad, flat forehead that formed a sharp ridge for bushy eyebrows; the high cheekbones and the thin, almost hawkish nose; the razor-edged jawline. All encased in that tawny skin that made him look healthy and robust even on the rare occasions when he wasn't.

Holding the orange crate against his hip, he slammed the trunk lid closed and took long, purposeful strides toward the house.

That managed to unfreeze Beth in a hurry. She let go of the curtain and nearly jumped back from the window so as not to be caught spying.

But she could hear his every step on the courtyard tiles and each one seemed to fall on a separate beat of her heart.

Remember you're divorced. And for good reasons. That's how you wanted it. That's how he wanted it....

When he rang the doorbell, it seemed to echo all around her. Fleetingly she considered not opening it, sparing herself the effect of having him at close range. Why couldn't he have just left well enough alone?

But Shag Heller's daughter couldn't be a coward, at least not more than she'd already been, and when the bell rang a second time she finally opened the right half of the door.

That was when he took off his sunglasses and she had to look up into the face that his grandfather couldn't have sculpted to more rawboned perfection. Eyes the color of coal homed in on her and she saw a muscle along the side of his powerful neck flex and unflex, warning her that he was not happy. To say the least.

"Hello, Ash," she greeted, as if letting him know from the get-go that she would give no quarter, even though just the initial sight of him was already awakening things inside of her that she didn't want awakened.

He didn't respond. He merely stood there, glaring at her.

She pretended not to notice, stepped aside and said, "Come on in."

He folded the temples of his sunglasses by pushing them against his chest. Then he slipped them into the breast pocket of his shirt. She had a little trouble removing her gaze from that wide expanse when he'd finished.

He swung the orange crate around in front of him, and that distracted her. But appreciating the hard muscles in his forearms, and his thick wrists and big, capable hands, didn't improve what was already thrumming in the pit of her stomach.

She forced her focus in the direction of the orange crate. "What's all that?"

"Things you left behind," he said, breaking the silence with a cutting tone in his deep voice. "You forgot some clothes at the cleaners and a few things that were in the extra closet."

But some of what she could see didn't qualify for either of those categories. They were things she'd purposely omitted from her suitcase.

She waggled a finger in that direction. "Those on top are yours. Even though I wore them, I sort of thought divorce reverted them back to you."

"I considered them yours."

Did that mean that once she'd used them, they were contaminated and he didn't want them back? Or that he still wanted her to have them?

She didn't know. And was afraid to find out. So she just said, "You can set the crate in the corner."

While he did, she closed the door and headed for the living room, sitting on one of three couches that formed a U around the big-screen TV, hoping she looked nonchalant.

Her former husband followed her, but he stayed standing, facing her from behind the opposite sofa, watching her as if it were dangerous to take those dark, penetrating eyes off her.

He folded his arms over his chest. "Talk to me," he ordered.

"I said everything in the letter."

"Not everything. You failed to tell me how it is that it took five months for you to let me know you're pregnant."

"Oh, don't get on your high horse about that. I didn't know it myself until a few weeks ago."

"How is that possible?" he challenged. "If you're five months gone, you were pregnant even before you filed for divorce."

"What are you thinking? That I knew and kept it to myself until after the divorce was final?"

His silence and one raised eyebrow answered her.

"Well, that's not how it was. I was so harried with tax season, and there was all the tension of the divorce, and you know I was never...regular...that I could skip a month or two and not have it mean anything..."

Somehow discussing the very personal issues of this subject suddenly seemed terribly awkward. She knew it was crazy. This was a man she'd shared the most intimate details of her body and its functions with for five years. But she was acutely aware of the fact that he wasn't her husband anymore. They were just two separate people now.

Still, there was no way around it.

She cleared her throat and forged on. "You also know we were using birth control. The fact that it might have failed just didn't occur to me until I really sat down and figured out exactly how long it had been since...I'd had a cycle. I finally went to see Cele and she ran a pregnancy test."

"Which was when?"

"Three weeks ago. I tried to see you. I went to your office, but Miss Lightfeather couldn't work me into your schedule." She bit off the cutting edge in her own voice. "Then I tried calling, but she said you'd been busier than usual and had a lot on your mind, so she hadn't relayed my messages. Your grandfather was out of town, I never seemed to be able to catch you at his house, and then Miss Lightfeather said you'd been called away, too. I was all packed by then, so—" Her voice had risen and the words tumbled out faster and faster, and Beth took a breath to slow it all down and retrieve the dignity she felt was slipping. "So I came home. I called a few more times and then just wrote," she finished flatly.

"Miss Lightfeather and I are going to have a serious chat."

"She's just keeping your priorities in order."

He ignored that comment. "Are you all right? Is the pregnancy normal? Healthy?"

"Everything is just fine. There was honestly no need for you to come here. I think I have the whole thing under control."

But even she heard the hedging in that. To hide it, she expounded. "You know that financially I'm in good shape. Even though Shag's will gave a quarter share to his lady friend—or whoever Ally Brooks is—what's left for Linc, Jackson and me to split is substantial. I'll be doing the accounting and investments for the three of us now, but that'll be my only job, so I can work right here and be a full-time mother. I know how you felt about us having kids of our own and this doesn't have to change anything for you. I'm willing to have and raise the baby on my own, and you don't even have to acknowledge it."

"As if I'd be happy to hear that!" he shouted.

It made her sit up a little straighter, a little stiffer.

"You know, sometimes you take being self-sufficient too damn far," he said through clenched teeth.

"It isn't a matter of being self-sufficient. It's just that I know this isn't what you'd planned, and I want to make it clear that it doesn't have to interfere—"

"No matter what I wanted or planned, it doesn't mean I don't want this baby now that it's on the way. Or that I'll let you treat me like a nameless, faceless sperm donor whose part in this is finished."

"I thought you'd be happy to be absolved of—"

"Well, you were wrong!"

She didn't like being yelled at and she suddenly found herself out of her seat, around the back of her own sofa, faced off against him. "Don't scream at me."

"Screaming at you is the least of what I'd like to do," he shouted. "You think I don't know that you want me to just disappear? That you'd like to believe you don't need me and you sure as hell don't want me? But this is one thing you're not doing on your own, damn it. This is my baby as much as it's yours."

"I never said it wasn't. I'm the one who repeatedly ran up against the brick wall of your schedule trying to let you know it *is* your baby, remember?"

"And that's as far as you figured to let it go? Tell me and then write me off while you do everything yourself—Superwoman?"

"What exactly is it that you think you can do? Carry this baby for the next four months? Give birth to it?"

That stopped him cold. For a time he merely stood there, his dark eyes boring into her, and Beth suffered a terrible warring between recognizing the pure magnificence of him and wanting him out of her life before that recognition could have too much effect on her.

"I don't know what we're going to do," he admitted. "What I do know is that for the first time this isn't just your business or responsibility, or just my business or responsibility. It's ours. And we're going to work it out together."

"There's nothing to work out. I'm going to have the baby, and after it's born if you want visitation—"

"You are not going to do that to me," he said, once more through clenched teeth, stabbing one long index finger her way. "You are not going to exclude me from this."

"What do you propose, then?" she rephrased her earlier question, feeling her own temper rise at the increasing possibility that he wouldn't just go away and leave her alone, that he wouldn't be satisfied with what she had in mind to keep her distance from him.

"All I know is that I'm going to be a part of this. From this minute on, any way I can. We made this baby together, we're going to have it together, and one way or another, we're going to at least collaborate to raise it together."

"Collaborate," she repeated. "Let me guess, you're going to have Miss Lightfeather fax me instructions on breast feeding."

His eyes narrowed at her and though it didn't seem possible, they grew even darker. "For now I'm not leaving Elk Creek. I'll take today to do what I need to to free up some time and then I'm dogging your every step until you and I have hashed through this and I'm satisfied with what my place in this baby's life will be."

Beth's initial reaction was to argue. She didn't want him within a hundred miles of her, let alone *dogging* her every step. It was too easy for old feelings to be rekindled, for her to lose sight of why they'd divorced, and fall under the spell of the attraction that had put them together to begin with.

But then she realized she was being foolish.

He wouldn't stick around long, no matter what he said. For the entire time she'd known him, something had been coming up to take him away. She had only to wait him out. Before she knew it, there would be a meeting he couldn't reschedule or a problem he couldn't ignore, and he'd be gone.

"Suit yourself," she said with complete confidence.

He continued to study her, as if he were suspicious of her agreement. But after a moment he merely said, "I'll be back. And don't even think about running out like you did last night, because I'll find you if it takes every dime I have."

"It won't be me who leaves," she said caustically and somewhat under her breath.

If he heard it, he chose not to address it. Instead, after another moment of piercing her with his heated glare, he turned and walked out the way he'd come in.

Beth hated that her gaze followed along, slipping down the expanse of his shoulders to the sharp narrowing of his waist, feasting on the sight of a derriere to die for. But follow along it did.

Only when he went through the front door and shut it behind him did she close her eyes and set her teeth together in determination.

He had a right to the baby and she wouldn't deny him that right.

But she'd be damned if she'd let him get to her. She'd ignore him. She'd go on about her business as if he weren't around. She'd find a way to keep herself removed from him, emotionally if not logistically.

And if, deep down, there was a tiny flicker of relief, that she might not be as alone in this as she'd thought?

She didn't want to admit it.

Not even to herself.

Chapter Three

As Ash showered and dressed early the next morning, he told himself to get a grip. Being mad at Beth didn't serve any purpose, and arguing with her, shouting at her, upsetting her, couldn't be good for the baby.

It was just that he was so damn frustrated!

He knew her, knew she'd go to any lengths to do this alone. Hadn't she sat there smugly and challenged him to tell her just what he thought he could do to be a part of things right now?

Of course he hadn't an answer. Pregnancy was a woman's domain. But he knew for certain that if he didn't make a stand now, if he didn't get involved in whatever way he could, then he'd never be a part of the baby's life once it was born, either.

But how long would it take to make his stand, to be truly involved? he asked himself. The baby wouldn't be born for four months. And there was no way he could put everything on hold with the foundation for that long.

Still, he could manage it for a little while. At least until he felt he'd established with Beth that he'd accept nothing short of his full role as father to this child.

And even then, when he went back to the reservation, he'd still have to find some way to keep in close contact with her, because he wanted to be in on this whole thing. It aggravated him that he'd already missed five months.

Although that aggravation couldn't have surprised him more.

Beth was right. He hadn't wanted them to have kids of their own. The days when there were a surplus of babies in the world to adopt might be all in the past, but there were still those who were hard to find homes for—babies born with handicaps, with fetal alcohol syndrome or drug addictions. The Native American community had many such children, who often had to be placed with families outside the culture.

Ash was among those who didn't like to see that happen, both because he believed Indian children should be raised knowing their heritage, and because recent programs attempting to reclaim children already outside that circle struck him as painful business for everyone involved. So he'd decided that when the time came for him to become a parent he wanted to do what he could to keep at least a few of those kids from being adopted out to non-Indian parents in the first place.

But that didn't mean he was going to turn his back on his own child. Beth was out of her mind to think he might. It was more than just doing the right thing.

This was *his child*.

There was something incredible about that. About the fact that he'd created a human being. Before, when he'd made his decision to build his family through adoption, he hadn't considered it any big deal to have a child of his own.

But he'd been wrong. It was a very big deal.

He was bowled over by the pure wonder of it. This child was *his*....

Would it look like him? Would it look like Beth? Would it have his paternal grandfather's artistic talent and give the world more that was beautiful and meaningful? Would it have his maternal grandfather's wisdom and kindness and irrepressible sense of humor?

It was just so damned amazing.

And he hated this feeling he had of being on the outside looking in.

There was no doubt about it, he was determined to be a force in this child's life. A presence as strong as Beth's. Even though he wasn't exactly sure how he was going to do that when he was divorced from the baby's mother and living on the other side of the state.

But he'd find a way, he vowed to himself. He would definitely find a way.

"Not through anger and confrontations like yesterday's, you won't," he told himself.

He knew he needed to forget that he'd already lost five months of this pregnancy. He needed to forget that Beth was doing her usual best to make him incidental. He needed to stop thinking that maybe if she had paid enough attention to what was happening in her own body and realized before the divorce was final that they were going to have a child, they might not have gone through with it in the first place....

But regrets about the divorce were useless. Hadn't he been telling himself that since the day it was final?

He'd be, more or less, a single father. And he'd just have to make every precious moment with his child count.

And yet, there was something very lonely about that idea. So lonely it was like a fist in his gut.

The picture his mind should have been conjuring up was of Beth and him standing together over the crib. Or of both of them watching the baby splashing in the tub. Or of their taking turns rocking it or walking the floors with it through the night...

"Well, that's not how it is. Or how it's going to be, so get over it," he ordered himself, trying to shake off the anger and those regrets he'd been fighting.

It wasn't easy, though. Nobody could get to him the way Beth could.

Good and bad.

And it didn't help that some of the good was still there.

Even in the midst of his rage at her yesterday, he'd still been drawn to her.

He'd watched her walk into the living room ahead of him and his hand had itched to reach out and touch her.

He'd remained standing behind the couch, hoping that distance and the barrier would keep things in perspective for him, when his damn brain had suddenly kicked in with images of what she looked like after they'd made love—all soft and warm and heavy lidded; of what she tasted like when he kissed her naked shoulder and found her slightly salty from the mingling of his sweat and hers from the heat of the moments just before; of what it felt like to be inside of her, to have her hold on tight to him, wrap her legs around him, cry out his name...

How the hell could he be so mad at her and hungry for her at the same time?

But he had been.

He was.

Wanting her didn't change anything, though, and he knew he had to keep himself focused on the future, not on the past.

The baby was all he needed to think about. And carving out his place with it.

He had no business at all thinking about his wife.

His ex-wife.

And that distinction was something he'd better not forget.

Beth had a lot planned for that day, but she was having a hard time getting herself going. She'd made it as far as into her bathrobe and downstairs to fix herself a cup of tea, but that was it. Here it was, late in the morning, and she was back in bed, still sitting propped on her pillows, staring into space.

Well, not exactly into space.

She was staring at that orange crate Ash had left the day before. She'd carted it upstairs after he'd gone and set it on the floor in the corner.

She might have just put the whole crate in the trash except that she knew the things she'd forgotten at the dry cleaners were some of her best. The trouble was, to get to them, she had to go through those items that really belonged to Ash.

Why hadn't he just kept them? Or thrown them out, if he hadn't wanted them back? Surely leaving them behind had made it clear she didn't want them.

Except that she sort of did.

It was just the memories that went with them that she didn't want.

But neither the crate nor the memories were going away, and she'd been sitting there much too long willing them to. She knew she was being silly. And silliness was another of those things that Shag would never have allowed in this house.

"Just pull out the stuff that's yours and then put the crate and the rest of it in the trash out back," she told herself as if there were nothing to it.

Pretending that that was the truth, she got out of bed, crossed the room, knelt down beside the offending box in the corner and quickly took the four top items off, setting them aside without more than a cursory glance at them.

"See? You were making a mountain out of a molehill."

What was left in the crate was a silk suit and a blazer still in the cleaner's plastic. She took them out and hung them in her closet. Then there were several items of winter clothing she'd kept in the bedroom of the house on the reservation that would have been the nursery. Those she stuffed into the bottom drawers of the bureau that faced the bed.

And that was that. She had only to toss those first few articles back into the crate, get rid of it, and she could be done with this whole business.

But was she sure she really wanted to just throw those things away? her traitorous mind asked her as she bent over to pick them up.

There was a great big, plaid cashmere bathrobe that was so old and worn around the edges that it wasn't even fit to give to charity. And yet when her hands clasped the downy softness, she couldn't resist fingering it, rubbing her palms against it, finally slipping it on, smoothing the ragged lapels over her chest.

She'd replaced it for Ash their first Christmas together, but when she'd been about to throw it out the next day she hadn't been able to. It had occurred to her that if she got rid of it she wouldn't have it to wear on cold Sunday mornings when she was padding around in her pajamas and stocking feet, or to pull over her when she was sick and lying on the couch.

There was something comforting about it in a way her own robe didn't match. It wasn't just that it was warm or soft or broken in; it always made her feel as if Ash himself were wrapped around her.

Just like now...

"This has to go," she said firmly, shrugging out of it as if it made her itch and tossing it into the crate.

Then there was his college sweatshirt.

She thought he would have wanted that back for sure. After all, it was a memento of his fraternity.

For Beth, on the other hand, it was a memento of something else.

The first time she'd worn it had been during a game of Boat.

Boat was something she'd heard a therapist on the radio suggest to a caller with marital problems. Beth hadn't considered what was happening in her own marriage a problem at that point—after all, it had only been a month since their wedding. But the game had seemed like a way to lure Ash home from doing paperwork at his office on a Sunday afternoon.

The instructions were to gather special foods and wine and maybe some body oils or lotions in a basket. Thus equipped, the basket was then to be taken to the bed, which was designated as a boat in the middle of the ocean, and, for a time, they couldn't leave it for any reason.

Ash had been only too happy to go along with the idea. He'd undressed her and flung her clothes far out into their imaginary sea. After they'd put the lotions and oils to good use, the only article of clothing she could reach when she'd wanted to dress again before their picnic had been his college sweatshirt.

That sweatshirt had become a part of the Boat basket from then on.

Unfortunately Boat had lost more and more of its power to bring Ash home as the years had gone on, until Beth had given up trying. Still, the memory of that first time was so sweet it hurt.

She folded the sweatshirt and set it in the crate with the robe.

A white dress shirt was the third item lying on her bedroom floor at that moment. It had become hers during a long business trip Ash had taken early in their marriage. He'd left it for her to launder. But when she'd tried to do that, the scent of it had reached out to her. Ash's scent. That mingling of his clean, spicy after-shave and the masculine smell of his skin.

She'd ended up not washing it at all, but wearing it around the house to stave off the loneliness.

It surprised her a little that he'd known to bring it to her. It was a plain white shirt, like so many of his others, except that it had a tiny flaw in the weave of the cuff. From that trip on, she'd kept the shirt, laundering it only when she knew he was about to leave again and slipping it in with his other shirts so that he'd wear it just before, infuse it with his scent, and then she'd have it after he'd gone.

"He knew all along," she whispered, embarrassed that he had realized what she was doing.

He'd never let on that he was aware the shirt appeared in his drawer only periodically before disappearing again.

But obviously he'd known that she'd considered it *her* shirt.

On their own, her hands brought it up to her nose and she breathed in the faint lingering of what had comforted her before. But there was no comfort in it now. There was only a terrible pang for what was lost.

She folded it with the care of a soldier folding a burial flag and set it in the crate.

That left the pajama top. Ash's pajama top.

From the beginning of their marriage he'd worn the bottoms and she'd worn the tops of every pair he'd owned during their years together.

Technically, she thought, they were as much her pajamas as his. He'd never worn this half.

Yet somehow, the day the divorce was final, she'd decided to put away that portion of the pajamas they'd shared along with the life they'd shared. So when she'd taken off her wedding ring, she'd also removed these pajama tops from her drawer and set them in one of his.

Unfortunately, since then she'd been trying to find something else she liked as well to wear to bed.

Women's pajamas, T-shirts, nightgowns, nightshirts. She'd even tried sleeping in the nude. But nothing was as comfortable as the silk pajama top she held in her hands at that moment.

"I bought them," she said. "Think of it as him wearing the bottoms of *my* pajamas."

But she wasn't sure she could.

And yet she also couldn't seem to make herself put them into the orange crate.

Lord, what was wrong with her? She'd never been so indecisive, so sentimental, so emotional.

And then it occurred to her that maybe more than her appearance could be under the influence of pregnancy hormones.

Of course, that was all it was, she told herself. The roller coaster emotions were caused by the increased hormones in her body. She even remembered reading something about that very thing.

But could they turn her into a different person? For here she was, Shag Heller's daughter, crying over a pair of pajamas, of all things.

Well, regardless of the cause, she could fight it, she decided. She *had* to fight it. She wasn't so weak willed that it could get the best of her.

She snapped the pajamas through the air with one hard flick as if that would rid them of the baggage they came with, spun away from the orange crate and stuffed them into her drawer, slamming it shut so firmly that it set the clock on top of the bureau rocking back and forth.

Twenty minutes to twelve? She couldn't believe it. And there she was, not even showered yet.

Enough mooning, she told herself, turning toward the bathroom that connected to her room.

She'd throw the clothes out later.

But somewhere in the back of her mind a little voice called her a liar.

And she knew it was right.

Especially when she took a detour and slid the crate into the back of her closet.

An hour later, Beth finally went downstairs, showered and dressed in a sleeveless, oversize chambray shirt with tails that reached nearly to her jean-clad knees, her hair freshly washed and fluffed. She intended to go straight out the front door and make her first stop Kansas's country store to see if by some chance her old friend might not have had lunch yet and could be persuaded to join her. But she only made it as far as the bottom step before spotting Ash sitting in the living room watching for her.

She couldn't believe it.

She'd never known him to actually free up time before, so she hadn't really taken his threat to do it now too seriously. At the most, she'd expected that he might do business from his cabin at the lodge for a few days, popping up once or twice in the evenings before being called away again.

But there he was, in the middle of the day, with a cup of coffee in one hand, an open briefcase on the table in front of him, a file folder in his lap and papers scattered around as if he'd been there for a while already.

"Morning. Not that it still is. Have you been upstairs asleep all this time?" he greeted amiably.

But Beth was not feeling amiable about his being there. Nor was she going to admit that she'd been awake but crying over his old things. "What are you doing here?" she demanded ungraciously as she crossed to the living room.

"Exactly what I said I was going to do. My calendar is clear and I'm all yours."

Her heart took a wild skip at that but she tamed it in a hurry. He hadn't been all hers when they were married, he certainly wasn't now. "This is crazy. You're a busy man, I don't need or want a shadow, so why don't you just get in your car and—"

"I'm not going anywhere," he told her with enough finality to end her rebuttal. He scooped all the papers into the file, deposited it in the briefcase and closed it with a

loud snap that seemed to seal the end to the argument.
Then he stood.

And she wished he hadn't.

He had on a black T-shirt that smoothed across his
broad shoulders and stretched so far around his biceps
that the seams were strained. Gleaming against the mock
turtleneck just below his throat he wore a talisman he was
never without—a burnished copper eagle arrowhead
hanging from a thin black cord. His stomach was perfectly flat beneath the taut knit, and when her gaze
drifted down that washboard hardness she found a pair
of tight, faded blue jeans.

No one could do for a pair of jeans what Asher Blackwolf could.

They rode low on his narrow hips and cupped his every
bulging muscle like a second skin. Beth had always loved
the way jeans looked on him, though she didn't get to see
the look often because he didn't spend a lot of time
dressed that casually. Maybe part of the reason she liked
it so much was that those rare occasions meant she really
did have him all to herself.

But she didn't *want* him all to herself anymore, she reminded herself. She couldn't.

"What's on your agenda today? You looked as if you
were headed out," he said, drawing her attention away
from his appearance.

"I have errands to run," she answered, her words
clipped and her irritation sounding.

"Great. I'll drive."

"*Shopping* errands," she said, upping the ante. "You
know, the kind of thing Miss Lightfeather does instead
of you?"

He ignored the barb and repeated, "I'll drive."

"This is ridiculous. The things I have to do today will bore you to tears and they don't have anything to do with the baby." Well, that wasn't exactly true, but the errand she needed to run that *did* have a connection to the baby was not one she wanted Ash's company on—she needed maternity bras.

"You're not getting rid of me, Beth."

"There just isn't a point to this," she insisted, exasperated by his stubbornness. "How about if I agree to start sending you a newsletter? I'll write once a week, tell you about every ache or pain or twinge I have, keep you completely updated. You'll know as much about my heartburn as I do. It'll be the same as being here, only you can go on about your business and so can I."

His expression said he was annoyed with her, but he merely tilted his head and stared at her out of the corner of his eye. "I'll drive," he repeated yet again.

The way he'd angled his chin had given her a view of the fading bruise left by Jackson's punch, and the sight of it made her feel slightly guilty. It cut short the argument that was bubbling inside of her. He wouldn't be around long anyway before something called him away, she reminded herself. "Oh, fine. But don't say you weren't warned."

For the second time that day she spun on her heels, heading for the door ahead of him. But his legs were much longer than hers and they reached the door at the same time, with Ash bending over her to open it before she could.

Did he think being pregnant made her incapable of opening a door for herself, for crying out loud? But more than the courtesy, what irked her was that when he got that near to her she could smell his after-shave and it went right to her silly head.

"How about some lunch?" he asked as they walked to his car.

"I'm not hungry," she snapped, because it was true. The man irritated her so much she'd lost her appetite.

"Hungry or not, you need to eat. You're skin and bones," he decreed as he held the car door for her, too. "It looks like somebody better pay some attention to what you're doing to yourself and my baby."

Beth merely glared at him as he ordered her to buckle her seat belt and closed the door.

Their first stop was at Margie Wilson's café, where Ash canceled Beth's order of a sweet roll and coffee and instead insisted she be brought a turkey club sandwich, a salad and a glass of milk.

Beth seriously considered letting the food sit there and rot, but by the time it arrived, her appetite had returned, too, and she ate.

Besides, it was served by Margie Wilson herself, who always fussed over her, and Beth wouldn't have hurt the other woman's feelings for the world.

"I see she carries more weight with you than I do," Ash observed when the café owner left them alone after actually persuading Beth to drink some of the milk he'd ordered.

"Margie is a nice lady. And I've always felt bad that my father didn't do right by her."

Ash's eyebrows rose in curiosity as he chewed a bite of his hamburger.

Beth wasn't fond of sitting in silence, so she elaborated. "Shag kept company with her for years. Not openly. He believed that it was wrong for Linc, Jackson or me to ever see him with a woman other than our mother—"

She stalled a moment, thinking that she understood that notion now, because she didn't at all like the idea of her child seeing Ash with another woman.

Or of her seeing him with one, either, for that matter...

She pushed the thought and the feelings that came with it away and went on. "But everyone in town—including me and my brothers—knew that Margie had back-door visits from Shag for years. We all thought that eventually—probably when we were grown—he'd marry her."

"But instead he took up with the mysterious lady friend in Denver," Ash surmised, fitting a piece of the puzzle.

"Ally Brooks," Beth confirmed. "At least that's who we think she is. He never referred to the woman he spent time with there as anything but his 'lady friend,' so we don't really know for sure. It's just a good bet since he left her an equal share of the house, the ranch, the oil rights, all the stocks and bonds and other assets. We all figured we'd finally get to meet her at the funeral, but you know about that."

"Mmm," Ash said as he swallowed. "I know it hurt you that the orders in his will were for you and your brothers not to be notified of his death until after he was already buried in Denver."

"It didn't *hurt* me," she denied, raising her chin in the air, because a Heller never admitted to such a thing. Even if it was true.

Ash just shook his head as if he knew better and something about it saddened and aggravated him at the same time.

But rather than go into it, Beth launched into small talk about this Ally Brooks person not answering any of

Jackson's attempts to contact her to buy her out of the ranch.

That managed to fill the time until they finished eating and she could finally put her attention into her errands.

Saying goodbye to Margie Wilson, Beth headed up Center Street at an energetic clip. She greeted Elk Creek's citizens, gazed in windows and basically did her shopping. And as she did, she tried hard to ignore Ash.

But having him along was a pain in the neck.

It was as if he didn't know what to do with himself and this leisure time. He merely followed her like a shadow, not even looking around, and driving her absolutely to distraction with his overbearing coddling.

He didn't want her bending over to try on the shoes she was shopping for to wear to Linc and Kansas's wedding. He didn't want her carrying a single bolt of cloth in the fabric shop where she needed material to make a dress for herself. In the drugstore he didn't want her reaching to the top shelf for the shampoo she needed. He didn't even like her walking as fast as she walked and he wanted her to stop and rest every hour on the hour.

And opinions! The man had an opinion on everything.

The heels on the shoes she wanted were too high. She shouldn't have the clasp on her watch fixed, she should just buy a new one. The flowered pattern on one fabric was too big, while the dots on another were too bright.

Even the lace she wanted for Kansas's gown was deemed not elegant enough and he'd picked out another, more expensive one and paid for it himself to make sure he got his own way in that, too.

By the time they reached the maternity shop at five, Beth was ready to punch him herself and it occurred to her that their marriage might have ended a lot sooner if he *had* spent more time with her.

"I need to go in here alone," she told him in no uncertain terms, not happy to find his interest apparently piqued for the first time as he peered in the window that displayed not only maternity clothes but also Elk Creek's only selection of baby furniture.

"I don't know why," he said, dismissing her claim.

"Just please wait out here."

"Give me one good reason?"

"What I need in here is none of your business."

"Seems to me this is the only place we've been today that *is* my business."

"Look," she said, anger ringing in her voice, "I've put up with you and your ideas on everything today, but this is where I draw the line. What I need in here is *underwear* and I don't want an audience when I buy it."

The corners of his mouth crept up into a maddening smile. "I've been with you when you bought *underwear* before, Beth," he said, mimicking her. Then he bent so close to her ear that she could feel the warmth of his breath against her skin and added, "I've even seen you in it, remember?"

Oh, she remembered all right. Things she didn't want to remember. Like plunging, lacy red teddies and sheer black sets that left nothing to the imagination. Unfortunately, she also remembered where wearing them led....

But those days were long gone. She ignored the heat she could feel in her face. "I have a right to some privacy."

He chuckled at that and she wondered why it was that she'd never noticed before how annoying he could be. He might be glorious to look at, standing there with that snow-dusted black hair, his gorgeous face relaxed with amusement and his arms crossed over his broad chest, but he was still insufferably smug. If he were one of her brothers and this was fifteen years ago, she'd have doubled her fist and landed a right cross to that washboard stomach of his.

But he wasn't one of her brothers and it wasn't fifteen years ago and she'd never let him know he was getting to her. In any way.

"Never mind. I'll do this when I get rid of you." She took a step away from the shop door, but that was as far as she went before his hand caught her arm and stopped her.

"You'll go a long time needing underwear that way," he warned, still apparently amused by her.

Then he did the most horrible thing. His thumb rubbed slow, sensuous circles against her bare skin and red-hot sparks skittered all the way to her stomach.

It was the first time he'd touched her since the night she'd decided to get a divorce. And it was not heartening to discover there was still power in even such simple contact.

She meant to tear her arm away indignantly. But somehow the best she could do was shrug out of his grip.

"Come on," he said, as if he'd been left completely unaffected. "I'll look at baby furniture and you won't even know I'm in the same store."

Oh, she'd know all right. But for some reason she didn't even want to think about, she was suddenly, uncomfortably aware of just how tight her regular bras had become. In fact she felt as if her breasts might burst right out of the cups. She definitely needed new bras. Right now. Whether he was there or not.

"Fine," she muttered. "But you'd better steer clear of me."

"Absolutely," he assured with so much laughter in his tone she really did want to hit him.

But instead she yanked open the store's door and marched in ahead of him.

The shop took up two storefronts—one for the maternity clothes and the other for baby furniture and accessories like car seats, booster chairs, mobiles and just about anything else mother or child could need. Three-quarters of the wall between the two sections had been cut away at the center so though there was a separation, most of each store was visible to the other.

Beth weaved her way slowly through the racks of clothes, keeping an eye on her former husband to make sure he was doing as he'd said he would and staying on the furniture side.

He was. In fact he was so interested in reading a potty-chair box that he seemed unaware she was around at all. Reassured by that, she nabbed a saleslady and asked for assistance with bras.

Unfortunately, the saleswoman, one of the few people in Elk Creek she didn't know, happened to have a very loud voice. Beth had asked if bras existed that could expand along with her body so she wouldn't have to replace them again from now until the end of her pregnancy, and the woman's answering lecture might as well have been given over a loudspeaker.

Standing near the rack the woman had led her to, Beth shot a glance at Ash. This time his interest was not in potty chairs. It was on Beth. Specifically, on her breasts, as he apparently checked for evidence of the need for this particular new underwear. And to make matters worse, she felt the heat of his gaze like a blast furnace.

Damn him!

Damn the saleswoman!

Damn herself for responding to the appreciation in his expression and the awful memories of having more than his gaze on her and how good it had felt once upon a time!

"Thanks for your help but I'll just browse myself now if you don't mind," she said in a hurry, taking a step behind a turnstile as she spoke. And if her tone was abrupt and offended the woman, at that moment she didn't care. Her only concern was for stopping the loud talk of engorged breasts and ultrasensitive nipples, and escaping from Ash's view of exactly those two things.

Hidden behind the rack, Beth looked for a back door to slip out of so she could escape. There wasn't one and she had no choice but to tough this one out, too. But, Lord, how she wished she'd never come into this store! The fact that this errand had turned into one of the most embarrassing of her life seemed a direct result of Asher Blackwolf and his stubbornness.

Damn him anyway.

He was making her sorry she'd ever told him about the baby. He didn't have any business here. Not in Elk Creek. Not in this store. Not in her life. And she was going to tell him so, she decided as she searched for her size and snatched three bras off their hangers. She was going to tell him in no uncertain terms to get out of town, that she'd keep him informed about the baby, but that was as far as she would go with him and he'd better just accept it.

And if he didn't?

Then she'd leave. She'd pack up in the middle of the night and she'd disappear. She wouldn't even let her brothers know where she was so there was no risk of one of them telling Asher Blackwolf.

Damn him anyway!

But then she stepped from behind the turnstile and caught sight of him again.

And some of the steam fizzled out of her.

He wasn't watching her anymore. He was studying a crib. Very intently. Very seriously. Checking its sturdiness. Checking the movement of the side and how secure it was when it was up. Checking the width of the gaps between the spindled bars.

And there was something very touching about the big man so intent in thoughts of his child's safety that it gave her heart quite a lurch.

Damn him anyway...

It struck her then that he was going to love this baby, just the way she was. Just the way she already did. That no matter what he'd thought or said before, now that it was on the way, he really did want it.

He really did want to be included in it all. And she knew she had to accept that, in spite of her own feelings about him. Feelings she was just going to have to control. No matter how difficult that might be.

Because regardless of what was between them, she couldn't deny him the pleasure of planning for this baby any more than she could deny him the baby itself after it was born.

But she could keep hoping something would distract him or call him away, to ease the burden of those feelings for a man who no longer wanted her.

The saleswoman recovered from her pique at Beth's curt dismissal and returned to take the bras to the register. She was still in a bit of a huff, which subdued her enthusiasm and, thankfully, her voice, so that Beth managed to pay for her underwear without more embarrassment.

When the transaction was complete, the baby furniture seemed to call to her, too, and she joined Ash.

"I think we should buy this set, tie it to the roof of the car and take it with us," he informed her decisively over an oak dresser, crib and matching changing table.

"It's too soon for that. And even if it wasn't, until Linc and Danny move in with Kansas, there's no room for it all."

That wasn't exactly true, but it seemed viable. The truth was that something about the purchase made Beth feel uncomfortable.

It wasn't that she had any more than the usual concerns about carrying the baby to full term or delivering a healthy infant; this had more to do with Ash. With the awkwardness of their situation. With her unwanted and unrealistic wish that they were choosing furniture to put in the nursery of the home they'd share with their child instead of the house she shared with her brothers.

"I don't think it's too soon," Ash persisted, oblivious to her thoughts and lost in his own. "But if you don't like it, maybe I'll have it sent to my place."

Everything seemed to stand still for Beth. "Your place?"

"Sure. I'll need the whole setup, too. For when the baby is with me on the reservation."

Beth felt as if he'd hit her. Hard.

She could barely breathe, let alone respond to that. All she could do was turn and leave behind the store, Ash and the beautiful furniture while she dealt with the sudden harsh realization that he was right, that there would actually be times when she would have to hand over her baby to him.

Somehow, in all of her previous thinking, that hadn't occurred to her. She'd pictured the baby with her. She pictured Ash spending—at most—a few hours or an afternoon with it. Not actually taking it across the state for days or weeks or *months*...

Outside she took long gulps of air to fight off the tears and anger that were tearing at her insides like claws.

"Beth?" Ash came out of the store behind her, his voice and expression rife with concern.

She wanted to shout at him, to scream that this baby was hers, that he could visit with it but that he couldn't buy furniture and set up a nursery and take her baby away!

But of course the rational part of her knew he could. That he would. That being the father would not be limited to visits.

"Are you all right?" he asked with an edge of panic to his voice.

"I'm going home" was all she could say, heading off around him with no idea of how she was going to get there.

But for the second time Ash stopped her, taking both her shoulders in his big hands and bringing her face-to-face with him. "Are you sick? Do you need a doctor?"

"No!" she yelled, trying to yank free of his grip, but he was holding her too tight to manage it. "I just want to go home."

The concern in his features edged toward confusion, but she had no intention of enlightening him. What could she say, after all? That she was feeling selfish and possessive and couldn't bear the fact that this baby she was carrying might say its first word or take its first step during his time with it instead of hers? That the reality of sharing this child had just struck her like a ton of bricks?

"I just want to go home," she repeated.

"Then let's go," Ash answered, turning her in the direction of his car.

Neither of them said any more as they drove back to the ranch. Beth was lost in her own thoughts, her own regrets that this baby would be brought into such a complicated situation. By the time Ash pulled up in front of the house she wanted only to go in and be alone.

But he wasn't having any of that. He insisted that he wasn't leaving until he'd made sure she had a well-balanced meal and really was okay.

And so they fixed dinner together. Ash barbecued two steaks while Beth prepared a salad, a fruit cup and sliced bread, all in silence, punctuated with loud closings of cupboard doors and the clattering of dishes, glasses and silverware placed heavily on the kitchen table.

She could feel Ash watching her as if he thought she'd lost her mind and might run screaming into the night at any moment, but it didn't matter. She almost felt as if she *could* run screaming into the night at any moment.

"Are you going to let me know what I did wrong?" he finally asked as they began to eat.

"You didn't do anything wrong," she said, her tone belying the words.

"You always have a violent reaction to the suggestion of buying baby furniture, is that it? Is something wrong that you aren't telling me?"

"Everything is fine. Just drop it."

Still, his black eyes bored into her while he chewed a bite of steak. "Do you want this baby, Beth?"

Her own fork stopped halfway to her mouth as she stared back at him. "Of course I want this baby. Not having one of our own was your plan, not mine."

Both his bushy eyebrows rose at that. "You never disagreed with it. If you wanted to have a baby, why didn't you say so?"

"I didn't really think you'd ever find a big enough break in your schedule to work it in either way."

"But what if I had? Would you have just gone along with the adoption idea and resented it rather than speak up and tell me how you felt?"

"I didn't say I resented anything."

"You didn't *say* a damn thing."

She merely went on eating without saying anything now, either.

He frowned at her. "Did you get pregnant on purpose?"

"No, I didn't. I wouldn't do something like that, in the first place. And in the second place, why on earth would I have willingly gotten myself into what's a long, long way from being ideal circumstances to bring a child into?"

"But you do want it now that it's on the way?"

"I said I did."

"You just don't want to buy a crib for it."

He wasn't going to get her to admit to what had hurt her in that maternity shop. To let him know that the idea of his taking the baby to the reservation was a weakness she had, a vulnerable spot. No way. Never. Shag Heller's daughter knew better than that.

"It's just too soon," she repeated.

He went on watching her as if he knew she was lying but didn't understand why.

Beth wished he'd leave. That he'd take his finely chiseled bones and his penetrating eyes and his broad shoulders hugged by that tight T-shirt and get out of her kitchen, her town and her life once and for all.

He finished eating and pushed his plate away, resting his hands on the table where his fingers drummed against the top in a slow rhythm.

She stared at those hands with their long, blunt fingers and she had a flash of what they felt like against her bare skin. Against her breasts. Against her nipples that were erect and straining within the too-small confines of her bra.

And then she noticed something else.

She noticed that there was a very faint tan line on the third finger of his left hand where his wedding ring used to be. And two things struck her. One—that he must not have taken it off until recently, even though the divorce had been final for a long time.

And, two—that even though it might have been belated—or even reluctant—he *had* taken it off.

And that fact was yet another jab at her heart.

Of course it was unreasonable. They were divorced. She'd taken off her rings, certainly he had to take off his.

But somehow, looking at that bare finger, where she'd once placed his ring, where it had stayed throughout their marriage, was painful, and she felt tears well up behind her eyes.

As she fought them, he spoke again and she had the sense that he could see some of what was going on inside her, because his deep voice was very quiet, very solemn, raising the lid on more unwanted feelings. "I wish that, just once, you'd let me know what's going on with you. Did you ever think that I might be able to make even one thing easier if you did?"

She snatched up her plate and took it to the sink. "You could make things easier for me if you'd go back to the reservation and leave me alone," she said, meaning for it to be curt and cold, yet it came out softly, almost a plea.

She set her plate on the counter, but she didn't turn back to him. She stared down into the sink as pure weariness washed through her and splashed against the tension in her neck like tidal waves against rocky cliffs.

"Why can't you just go away?" she nearly whispered, digging her own fingers into her nape.

She heard his chair scrape back and the sound of his heels on the tile floor as he came up behind her.

He stopped very near and took her hands away to replace them with his, kneading the tension with strong, capable fingers that seemed to know the exact spot and the perfect pressure to ease the taut muscles and tendons.

Her gazillionth wish for that day was that it didn't feel so wonderful or work so well.

But it did, and little by little she felt herself relax beneath his expert ministrations, even leaning toward him until she was almost resting against the hard expanse of his torso.

"I only want to help," he said in a husky voice, just before he pressed a kiss to the side of her neck with warm lips.

And then, somehow, she was facing him, gazing up into his inscrutable eyes as his mouth lowered to hers, capturing hers in a kiss that had nothing to do with stress relief.

She knew this kiss well. The tenderness in it. The anticipation. The sweetness before the storm of passion. And more than being familiar, it awakened things inside her that had no business being awake. Desires. Yearnings. Cravings for what she knew could be so good between them.

But it was the only thing that was any good between them, and she also knew that indulging in it would only further complicate an already too-complicated situation.

Besides, deep inside she carried with her the vivid memory of the loneliness that had followed that last time they'd made love, the loneliness of her entire marriage to him. Nothing was worth revisiting that.

She pushed from his kiss, from his arms, sidestepped away from him and, without looking at him, said, "You'd better go."

He didn't move, but she could feel him staring at her again; she could feel his confusion, his anger. After a moment he said, "I'll clean up here first. You've had a long day. Put your feet up and watch some TV or go to bed."

It was a direct order, given in a voice tight with control. But Beth decided to obey it just to finally put the needed distance between them.

She didn't say good-night or thank him for lunch or dinner or clearing the mess. She simply straightened her shoulders and walked out.

Because to say anything else, to do anything else, to even raise her eyes to his one more time, could all too easily have put her back in his arms.

Where a part of her wanted much too badly to be.

Chapter Four

"Robert Yazzie here."

"That sounded very official, old man," Ash answered his grandfather's telephone greeting affectionately, when he reached the elderly Indian at the offices of the Blackwolf Foundation early the next morning.

Robert laughed as if he'd just pulled off a good joke. "It's this big chair of yours. Makes me feel like the president."

Ash had asked his maternal grandfather to oversee the foundation during his absence. Robert Yazzie was not a businessman, but he had common sense and an easygoing nature that let him handle things without panicking. Plus, Ash knew he wouldn't try tackling anything beyond figurehead status. And the elderly man enjoyed brief interruptions to his retirement.

"How's that bum knee of yours?" Ash asked, settling down on his unmade bed to talk.

"It's keeping me off the golf course or I wouldn't be making your apologies for you to all those people you're standing up," Robert answered with yet another laugh that made him sound as jolly as Saint Nick.

Ash had been raised by both his grandfathers, but his relationship with Robert was the closer of the two. He'd stayed with Robert the majority of the time, going to work with him on weekends and during vacations from school. As the less temperamental of the two grandfathers, Robert had seemed to enjoy having his grandson's company, and Ash had preferred to be with him, too.

It was Robert who had instilled in Ash the importance of family and Indian ways and community. But most of all, the old man was just plain fun to be around. His love of life was infectious. Ash counted him not only as grandfather, mentor and teacher, but also as his best friend.

"You aren't driving Miss Lightfeather too crazy, are you?" Ash teased him back, sitting against the headboard and swinging his feet onto the mattress to cross them at the ankle.

"I don't think that woman likes me," Robert confided in a lowered voice as if the secretary might overhear.

That made Ash laugh. "Miss Lightfeather doesn't like anybody."

"Except you. I think she had a crush on you. But I told her about the baby the way you wanted me to and it didn't sit well with her. She even asked me if I was sure it was yours, like she was hoping it wasn't."

"It's mine."

"That's what I told her and I got cold coffee the rest of the afternoon yesterday because of it."

"Don't let her get away with that. Be firm with her."

"Ha! She might hurt me."

Again Ash laughed. His grandfather was over six feet tall and weighed upward of two hundred pounds. Compared to that, even the pudgy Miss Lightfeather was a bantamweight. "How's everything else going?"

"Fine, but where is everybody? Don't you have a staff of some kind?"

"Not really, you know that."

"I knew you didn't have any full-time help, but I thought you at least had some part-time people. Nobody's been around but Miss Lightfeather and me."

"I don't schedule my part-timers regularly, only as I need them. I do as much as I can myself—or should I say, Miss Lightfeather and I do as much as we can. It cuts costs, and that way, rather than putting a lot of money in salaries, I can spread it around where it can do more good."

"Ahh. I've been hearing a lot about cost effectiveness and money, that's for sure," Robert said. From there the elderly Indian brought him up-to-date on the proceeds from a benefit dinner the night before to raise money for the homeless. He told him about a bequest that had been left to the foundation by a Native American woman who had just died, and related several other, smaller events, as well as news of the trial of the boy in Alaska whom Ash had hired legal counsel for.

"So how's our little Beth?" Robert asked when he'd finished.

Ash knew his grandfather and Beth were close. They'd shared interests in several things and Robert had taken her under his wing. "She's too skinny."

"That's not good. We're a family of big babies. She's going to need her strength and some meat on her bones when it comes time to deliver your son."

Ash smiled. "You're sure it's a boy, are you?"

"Just hoping. It's good to have a boy to carry on the name." Robert paused and then ventured cautiously. "Now that the shock has worn off, how do you feel about this?"

"A little giddy," he admitted what he wouldn't admit to anyone but his grandfather.

Robert chuckled. "Then you're not unhappy about it?"

"I've surprised myself by how excited I am."

"Babies will do that. There's something magical about them." This time Robert cleared his throat. "So, uh, what're you going to do about it?"

"What am I going to do about what?"

"Well, you know, babies have a right to be born into a loving house complete with a mother and a father."

"This one will be born into two loving homes, one with a mother and one with a father. It gets a bonus," Ash said, trying to make light of what he really didn't see that way.

"Is that how you want it?"

"We're divorced, Pap, that's just how it is." Ash didn't have to be in the same room with his grandfather to see him nodding his head in that sage way that accepted what he said and still managed to disagree with it.

"I surely do miss that girl," Robert said. "She plays a mean gin rummy. Haven't had as good a game as she gives me since she left."

"Are you telling me you're sorry she didn't get custody of you in the settlement?" Ash joked.

"Just saying I miss her. Thought you did, too, the way you were grumbling around here when you moved in. You sleepin' nights yet?"

"I sleep fine," Ash lied.

"And here I was thinking all those times I heard you up walkin' around were because your bed was too lonely without her."

"I've slept in plenty of beds without her."

"Humph. Maybe too many. Sometimes it seemed like she spent more time with me than she did with you."

"She never complained about it. But if you have something to say to me, old man, spit it out."

"Only thinking that with a baby coming now, maybe she'd take you back."

"She acts like she can't stand the sight of me."

"Must have kept her eyes closed to get that baby in her belly, is that what you're tellin' me?"

"She must have."

"So what're you doing there?"

"Claiming what's mine."

"The baby, you mean."

"The baby."

"Are you sure that's all that's yours? Maybe Beth could be, too, if you handled things right."

"Maybe you ought to come here and *handle* things and I should just stay on the reservation and run the foundation. I think she likes you better anyway."

"Maybe. We had some good times together, me and that little girl."

Ash said, "Look, Pap, I have to go. You have the number here at the lodge and the one at the ranch, in case you need me, right?"

"We'll be fine. Between Miss Lightfeather and me, we could run the world. It's Beth who needs you now."

"That'll be the day."

"Don't be too sure of it."

Ash exchanged goodbyes with his grandfather rather than comment on that and hung up, thinking as he did that if there was one thing he *was* sure of, it was that Beth Heller didn't think she needed him. For anything.

Except maybe making this baby. She hadn't been able to do that alone. And there was one other thing he was sure of, though he wouldn't have admitted it even to his grandfather. He was still more attracted to her than to any woman he'd ever met.

He leaned his head back and stared up at the ceiling, thinking about the night before.

He couldn't believe he'd actually kissed her.

After the day they'd had together, with her letting him know his very presence irked her, he'd kissed her, of all things.

And worse than that, he'd wanted to do a whole lot more than kiss her.

Old habits die hard, he told himself. That was all it was.

Sex had always been good. Toward the end of their marriage, it was the only time he ever felt close to her. The only time it seemed that he could reach her, understand her and what she wanted and needed and would accept from him. The only time he wasn't so damn frustrated by her.

In fact, making love to her had often been a way to overcome those other, less than pleasant feelings she'd raised in him. So last night, at the height of her confusing and frustrating him and making him feel helpless and useless and all the things he hated, he'd just naturally turned to what he'd always done before.

"Right. As if you weren't so hot for her you could have sizzled those steaks on your skin," he said out loud.

All right, it hadn't just been a response to other things. He'd wanted her.

She'd turned to face him and raised those big blue eyes to him, parted her lips in what had looked like an invitation, and at that moment—just as when they were married—nothing else had mattered.

And when he'd kissed her, she'd kissed him back. One hundred percent.

For a few moments, anyway. Before she'd ended it and acted as if she couldn't even stand to look at him.

The woman drove him crazy. She really did. He didn't know what the hell she wanted.

But he knew what he'd wanted.

He'd wanted to take her upstairs to the nearest bed and make love to her until neither of them could walk.

Ash swung his feet to the floor and jammed his hands through his hair in self-disgust at the fact that just thinking about kissing her flooded him with a fresh wave of desire.

But he knew he had to control it. She didn't want him. She didn't want anything to do with him. That was obvious. Hell, she hadn't even been able to pick out baby furniture with him.

It was just too bad her total contempt of him didn't cool things off inside of him.

Because it was pure hell to be burning up with wanting a woman who couldn't even tolerate him.

Beth was a little surprised not to find Ash there when she went downstairs around noon that day. She'd been down much earlier, having gotten up at the crack of dawn, fixed herself a light breakfast and then gone back to her room to work on Kansas's wedding dress. Of course he hadn't been around then. But she'd thought that on her second trip she'd probably find him waiting, the way he had been the day before.

Not that she wanted him to be.

But she'd thought his claim that he was sticking around would last more than one day before he answered some summons from somewhere.

Or maybe he'd been as shaken as she was by that kiss and it had convinced him that their being together was not a good idea. Maybe it had driven him back to the reservation all on its own.

And if she knew just a pang of disappointment at the thought that his time here had been so short-lived?

She beat it down like a spark in a hayloft.

If he had left Elk Creek, it was for the best, she told herself as she headed for the kitchen. It was just what she'd wanted. What she'd hoped for. Now she could concentrate on the baby and carving out a new life for herself back in her old hometown without giving Asher Blackwolf another thought.

In the kitchen she went straight to the refrigerator. But as she stood in the open door and looked at her choices for lunch, she realized that somewhere between her bedroom and here she'd lost her appetite again.

Maybe if she waited awhile, it would come back. Kansas was due for a fitting anytime now, and, once her friend got here and she had some company, she might be able to eat then.

As she closed the refrigerator door a loud clanging of metal hammering metal sounded from outside.

She hadn't realized Jackson was working nearby today and, grateful for the distraction, she went to the window above the sink to see what he was doing.

But out at the barn off the southwest corner of the house, her brother wasn't alone. And, to Beth's immense surprise, he wasn't the one working the forge and bellows to form a horseshoe. Ash was.

Beth couldn't have been more stunned if she were looking at the pope on a bucking bronco, for never had she seen her former husband do any sort of manual labor. Ash was a businessman through and through.

Or so she'd thought.

He'd hired Indian boys on the reservation to mow the lawn in the summers and shovel the snow in the wintertime, and men to paint the house and fix anything that needed it around the place.

And yet there he was, stripped to the waistband of another pair of hip-hugging blue jeans, doing the work of a burly blacksmith.

"Amazing," she whispered to herself as she absorbed the idea.

But the sight was pretty amazing, too.

Hot weather had definitely arrived on this last day of June. The temperature was easily in the nineties. The heat emanating from the forge was so intense she could see the wavy distortion in the air, and she marveled over the physical exertion that went with melding iron into shape. Sweat glistened over Ash's naturally bronzed flesh.

And it was something to behold.

There was a very primitive and purely masculine beauty in what her eyes feasted on. Hard, honed muscles in his shoulders, back and biceps rose and rippled and proved their power. Even the planes of his handsome face seemed sharper, the skin more taut over the chiseled bones.

For a few moments she watched in wonder as his big, black-gloved hands worked the forge bellows and then took the shoe to the anvil, where he wielded the hammer with a skill she hadn't known he possessed. But appreciation for his workmanship couldn't keep her gaze from sliding up the tensed tendons of his forearms, all the way to his back again.

As always, he wore his coarse, straight hair in a queue that reached to the middle of his spine, clinging to it and pointing downwards like a shaft and arrow to where two slight dimples winked at her from just above his jean pockets.

Holding the finished shoe in long pincers, he plunged the hot metal into a bucket of water, sending a loud sizzle through the air. Beth thought cold water thrown against her own skin at that moment might have made the same sound.

And something in the pit of her stomach knotted and twisted with yearning.

Her hands itched to glide along his ribs, to feel the power in his arms beneath her palms, to absorb the heat and the potency of him. She wanted to bury her face in the slight valley of his pectorals, to taste the saltiness of his flesh, to feel the hardness of those muscles against her softer parts, to kiss a path down the center line of his torso to his navel, and maybe lower...

And then, suddenly, there was a knock on the front door just before it opened and Kansas called, "It's me."

Beth was jolted out of her study of her former husband, and she struggled to find her voice through the tightness in her throat. "Come on in," she answered, hoping her old friend didn't hear the breathy undertone.

Her heart was racing; perspiration dotted her palms, and even knowing she was about to be caught in the act, she had trouble tearing her gaze from Ash. Instead, still staring, she turned on the cold water, dampened her hands and pressed cool, moist fingertips to her cheeks in an attempt to calm the color she knew flushed them.

"Where are you?" Kansas asked from what sounded like somewhere in the living room.

"The kitchen," Beth answered, snatching one last glance of masculine magnificence before she turned away from the sink and tried to look nonchalant.

Kansas came through the swinging door with a jaunty stride. A serene smile brightened her face. "Hi," she said, setting her purse on the countertop just inside the door.

Beth returned the greeting and took the few steps to the butcher block in the center of the room. She knew it was absurd, but she had the sense that her back was being scorched by the heat of the scene she'd been observing. "Have you had lunch?" she asked too eagerly.

"Just before I came. Linc and Danny brought burgers to the store so we could eat together. I'll sit with you while you have something, though."

But what Beth was really hungry for was not food and so she shook her head. "No, that's okay. I'm sure you want to get back to work. Why don't we just pin up that hem so you can?"

Apparently there wasn't evidence of what had been going on in Beth's mind moments before, because Kansas didn't seem to notice anything amiss. "If you aren't starving, that would work better for me. My sister is holding down the fort while I'm gone, but she has some other things she needs to do today, so I hate to keep her any longer than I have to."

"Let's go up and get to work, then."

Kansas talked about the weather and her general store's air-conditioning being on the fritz as they went upstairs, but Beth was concentrating on getting some control over herself.

In her room she tried to avoid the window as Kansas slipped out of her clothes and put on the dress, but somehow the sill was where she ended up perching, and more than once she stole glances down as Ash formed and fitted another shoe and Jackson looked on.

And though she hated herself for it, she had to fight a strong reluctance to leave that window and the sight of Ash.

But of course she forced herself.

While Beth pinned the hem, Kansas chatted about Danny and something funny the three-year-old had said. Beth barely heard her as her attention kept straying toward the window. Even though she couldn't see out of it from where she knelt at the base of the chair her friend stood on, she was acutely tuned in to every sound. So much so that she even knew the moment the last nail was hammered into the last shoe and the horse was led through the squeaky paddock gate.

"I must be boring you to death," Kansas said at about the same moment.

"No, no, I'm just a little drifty today," Beth assured her, not really knowing whether she'd missed something important or not.

"Are you feeling okay? Do you have morning sickness or anything like that?"

"I feel great," she answered, thinking that feeling hot and bothered and inappropriately aroused by the wrong man didn't count. Then she added, "I never had any morning sickness, even early on, or I might have realized I was pregnant sooner." But she didn't want to say much more about her pregnancy, knowing it was insensitive in view of the fact that her friend couldn't have kids.

Luckily she'd finished pinning the hem by then and so could change the subject naturally. "That's it. We're all set. You can take the dress off and get back to the store. I'll have it finished by tonight."

Kansas seemed in no hurry to get out of the gown and instead went to the cheval mirror in the corner to admire Beth's handiwork for a few more minutes before actually changing out of it again.

To make amends for her inattentiveness, Beth asked a number of questions about how the preparations for the wedding were coming. The effort helped to finally get her own mind off Ash, so that by the time they headed back to the kitchen to get Kansas's purse, she felt like herself again.

But it lasted only until they went through the swinging door and came upon Jackson and Ash.

The scent of clean, honest sweat was in the air and though Beth knew it was crazy, the fact that part of it came from Ash acted like an aphrodisiac on her, rekindling much of what she'd thought she'd conquered.

But there he was, standing in the same spot she'd been at the sink, washing his hands, and she had the awful urge to walk up behind him, wrap her arms around his narrow waist and do silky, sexy things to his bare back.

Greetings and small talk between Kansas, Jackson and Ash made her lack of participation unobtrusive as she struggled with the urge, but struggle she did.

Until Kansas invited them all to dinner that night.

"Sounds great," she heard Ash answer before she could refuse.

"I have a Cattleman's Association meeting," Jackson declined as he unburdened the refrigerator of ice tea and the fixings for sandwiches. "But you all go ahead without me."

"And that way you can bring the dress," Kansas added, sealing the date before Beth could manage to utter a word.

"I can bring the dress by without your having to cook," she said, belatedly trying to get out of what would be a social evening that coupled her with her ex-husband.

But by that point, Kansas wouldn't hear of their not going to dinner, and she was locked in.

"About seven," her soon-to-be-sister-in-law said as she slipped her purse strap over her shoulder.

Beth only smiled in answer, hoping it didn't look as wan as it felt.

Goodbyes were said all around. When Kansas left, Beth felt as if she'd been abandoned to the wolves.

Silly thought.

"Have you had lunch?" Jackson asked her then.

Just the idea of sitting a few feet away from Ash and his naked torso while she ate a sandwich was an exercise in agony. "I ate before Kansas got here," she lied to get herself out of it. She'd eat something after Ash was gone.

Ash was leaning his hips against the edge of the counter as he dried his hands and watched her. "What do you have planned for this afternoon?" he inquired, the first words he'd said directly to her.

"I'll be up in my room hemming the wedding dress," she answered in a hurry, hoping it would convince him to leave.

He nodded, pushed off the counter and went to the butcher block, where Jackson was building four enormous sandwiches. Ash swung a long leg over one of the bar stools there and the flash of his zipper as he did made Beth catch her breath.

"I guess we can shoe those other two horses, then," he told her brother.

"Great," Jackson said enthusiastically, clearly over his anger at his former brother-in-law.

Beth's gaze had taken a rocket leap and landed in the hollow of Ash's throat, where the arrowhead nestled against his skin. Hearing their plans, she wondered how she was going to get through the afternoon without gawking at him.

"I thought you were using preformed shoes," she said peevishly to her brother.

Jackson's expression told her he found her curt tone curious. "I have been. But the red mare has a bad foot and needs a special fit, and since we're all set up and Ash is willing, we might as well do it for the other two, too."

Dandy.

"Did you need me for something else this afternoon?" Ash asked her.

What flashed through her mind was not something she was about to share with him. "I'm hemming a dress," she repeated.

"Then it shouldn't matter if I work with the horses."

Both men apparently knew something was going on with her and, hating that she was so transparent, Beth drew herself up into a ramrod-straight posture and shrugged as if they were imagining things.

"It doesn't matter to me at all," she lied again, turning to leave.

About the time her hand reached the door to push it open, Ash said, "I'll go back to the lodge when I'm finished, shower and pick you up a little before seven."

Beth bristled, ignoring the faint tingle of excitement that ignited deep inside her at the same time. "No, thanks. I'll just see you there," she said firmly.

"I don't want you going out alone, late at night. I'll pick you up," he insisted.

"What could possibly happen to me? I'm only fifteen minutes outside of town."

Ash looked at Jackson and said, "You know, she's the most stubborn person I've ever met."

"Ha! You didn't know Shag very well then."

The exchange that excluded her only got her back up more. "Let's not be ridiculous about this. I'll drive myself to Kansas's house."

"I'll pick you up a little before seven."

She rolled her eyes and took a breath, shoring up to really let him have it.

But then she realized that arguing with him left her in that kitchen all the longer.

Besides, for some reason, this new quest of his to be a conscientious father made him far more stubborn than she was, and she knew he would take this to the wall rather than give in. It was better for her to concede, she decided, and escape.

"Oh, fine. Have it your way," she finally said ungraciously. Then she turned on her heels to leave.

But as she did, she knew that having Ash out by the barn, shoeing horses, was going to make for a long afternoon.

And she wasn't looking forward to the evening, either.

By a quarter to seven that night Beth felt more in control of herself again. It helped that Ash had been gone more than two hours and that she'd taken a cool shower.

It also helped that she'd found a logical explanation for the even more intense attraction she'd been feeling toward him since his arrival in Elk Creek. Pregnancy hormones might well be causing these strange physical reactions, as well as her overly emotional state.

It was possible, she'd decided, that some biological quirk drew a woman to the father of the child she was carrying as Mother Nature's way of uniting them in spite of whatever other circumstances might exist. And somehow, the thought that it was just one more thing to endure—like the weakening of her bladder—put a new perspective on it for her.

She'd just ride it out, she told herself. She'd use better judgment and common sense to keep a lid on it. And it wouldn't be long, she was still convinced, before Ash left anyway.

With this new outlook, she felt sure that even the evening she faced could be passed with no more involvement than if she and Ash were any two acquaintances having dinner with another couple.

And the fact that she'd dressed up for the occasion had nothing whatsoever to do with her former husband. She'd merely felt inclined to celebrate this new lease on things with an airy halter sundress that fit loose enough to conceal her stomach, lacy espadrilles, and her hair gathered into a small cascade of curls at her crown. Everything worked together to make her feel cool and confident, and that was her goal, she told herself. Not to be attractive to Ash.

She was watching for him when he drove up, so she could forestall his coming to the door. This wasn't a date, after all.

He was out of the car by the time she left the house and so he went around to the passenger side to open that door for her.

She said a cursory hello and let him take the wedding dress and lay it across the back seat while she got in the front.

Beth tried not to notice how good he looked as he rounded the car on his way to the driver's side. He was freshly showered and wearing a pair of gray slacks and a crisp white shirt with the sleeves rolled to his elbows.

This was the Ash she was familiar with—casually chic, the businessman out for an evening with friends. It was less heady than the sight of him earlier today had been, though one whiff of his cologne as he joined her in the car did make her stomach flutter.

Hormones, she reminded herself. Nothing more than hormones.

He didn't start the engine right away. Instead he turned in her direction, propped one elbow on his headrest and the other on the steering wheel, and took a slow appraisal of her from topknot to toe.

"You look wonderful tonight," he said when he was finished.

"Thanks," she responded as if the compliment didn't matter, when in fact it secretly pleased her no end.

"There really must be a glow that comes with pregnancy because you seem all pink and healthy and—"

"Maybe you just never took the time to notice before." The words were out before she had a chance to think about them, and before he could say anything she poked her chin in the direction of the key in the ignition. "Don't you think we ought to get going?"

"Sure," he said as if he didn't quite understand her attitude in response to courtesy and compliments. He faced forward and started the car. "I spoke to my grandfather this morning," he went on then, showing better manners than she had, she knew. "He's missing you as his gin rummy opponent."

Just the thought of Robert Yazzie softened her mood and made her smile. The old man was truly a gem. He'd kept her company, explained Indian customs, helped her to know where she could and couldn't go on the reservation so she didn't embarrass herself. He'd been more friend to her than in-law.

"I miss him, too. How is he?" she asked, hearing the distinct change in her own tone of voice.

"He's the same—full of life." Ash took his eyes off the road to glance at her. "You know, I was always a little jealous of what the two of you had between you."

The last thing she needed was for Ash to flirt with her, and she refused to encourage it, so she merely confirmed what he'd said. "We did have fun together. You must be more like your other grandfather." She hadn't meant that to be an insult, merely an observation, but it had sounded pretty bad. She tried for a quick recovery. "I mean—"

"I know what you meant," he said grimly.

It was clear she'd insulted him and it left her feeling very small and petty as the third strike seemed to end his attempt to make this evening pleasant.

But it wasn't only *this* evening, she thought as his attention turned to his driving and left her to consider her recent behavior toward him.

With the exception of that first day they'd seen each other and argued, he'd been working to keep things between them calm and easy for her. Even when she knew she'd annoyed him, he hadn't vented it; he'd merely turned his anger inward, like now. But she'd been acting like a spoiled child or some sort of prima donna.

Of course she had a good reason—anything was better than succumbing to her softer, warmer, sexier feelings for a man who didn't want her. But still, she wasn't proud of herself. Hormones or no hormones, roller coaster emotions or not, she wasn't handling things well and she vowed to curb the hostility she used like a shield.

Fighting the attraction she felt to him was no excuse for flinging all his efforts in his face or offending him. In the future she had to find a way to control her own feelings without being so prickly, or she wouldn't be able to live with herself.

Besides, she honestly didn't believe he'd be here for long and it seemed silly now to make it so miserable for them both. And she also realized that trying to establish a more amiable relationship would serve the two of them and the baby in the long run.

But they'd reached Kansas's house by the time she'd come to that conclusion, and Ash was out of the car before she'd thought of a way to make amends. She did, however, thank him for opening her door, venturing the first smile she'd allowed him since he'd been in Elk Creek.

Unfortunately, he didn't see it; his gaze seemed to go over the top of her head, as if that were the only way he could refrain from letting her know what he thought of her and her contrariness.

He took the wedding dress out of the back, and as Beth accepted it from him, she reconsidered an attempt to rectify things before they went inside.

"Look, I'm sorry," she tried on the way up the porch steps, but apologies were no easier for her than sharing any other feelings, and it came out sounding impatient and uncontrite.

"Forget it," he said as he rang the doorbell, still not looking at her, his own tone clipped as he stood there as straight and stiff as any cigar-store Indian.

And Beth couldn't help wondering if ever there were two people worse together than they were.

Before she could say any more, her nephew answered the door.

All two and a half feet of Jackson's same brand of solemn stoicism, Danny regarded them seriously, his big green eyes taking in Beth and then rolling slowly up the full length of Ash.

Linc kept Danny with him most of the time, either at the honky-tonk he was building or here at Kansas's house. When Ash had been at the ranch, Danny had either not been there, or been in bed asleep. This was his first sight of the big man.

Beth opened the screen. "Hi, sweetheart," he said to the little boy. "I'll bet you don't remember Ash, do you? You were barely more than a baby the last time your dad brought you to see us."

Danny stepped out of the way so they could go in; he stared at Ash the whole time. "He gots lo-ong hair," the three-year-old marveled.

"Hi, Danny. It's good to see you." Ash held out his hand to shake Danny's much, much smaller one, but Danny snatched his behind his back rather than let Ash touch him, and dived for Beth's side, where he wrapped his other arm around her legs as if he needed protection.

Ash only smiled, took something from his pocket and hunkered down on his heels so he was nearer to eye level with the little boy. "I brought you something," he said, upturning his closed fist and opening it. "An Indian arrowhead."

Danny merely frowned at Ash and then at the arrowhead lying in his palm.

Ash picked it up between two fingers and held it out to him in a way that it could be taken without there being any contact between them. "Just carrying it around with you makes you strong. See, I wear one all the time," he added, pulling his from inside his shirt.

That seemed to interest the little boy, who carefully reached for the arrowhead, comparing the polished stone to Ash's burnished copper.

"What do you say?" Beth urged gently.

"Thanks," Danny muttered. Then he let go of Beth's leg and made a beeline down the hallway that led to the kitchen, shouting for his father.

Kansas appeared at the doorway through which Danny had gone, wiping her hands on a dish towel. "Come on in," she said, before noticing the wedding gown Beth carried. When she did, she hurried to them instead. "Oh, I don't want Linc to see the dress. Let me take it upstairs."

She did just that, sending Beth and Ash into the kitchen, where they found Linc studying the arrowhead Danny seemed very impressed with in spite of his leeriness of the man who had given it to him.

Linc sent him out to play then and turned his attentions to Beth and Ash, and the evening got under way.

Danny's wariness didn't lessen through most of the dinner they ate on the picnic table in the backyard to escape the heat of the house. The little boy kept a close eye on Ash, warming up to him only at a snail's pace.

But by the time Linc rounded his son up to be put to bed in Kansas's guest room, the three-year-old had overcome his trepidation enough to make a muscle to show Ash the arrowhead was already working its magic.

While Linc was gone, Kansas, Beth and even Ash did the dishes. Then Linc came back and the four of them had dessert outside, too, settling into more of the easy conversation that was making it a pleasant visit.

It was after eleven before Beth knew it, and though she hadn't had much of a chance to prove to Ash directly that she intended to be nicer, things between them had eased her in that direction.

Linc and Kansas walked them out, their arms wrapped around the small of each other's backs, and Beth knew a sharp tug of regret that she and Ash didn't share that kind of closeness and affection. But she reminded herself that it was only the hormones causing her to envy them, probably coupled with the weariness that came with the late hour, and she forced the feelings away as they all went out onto the front porch.

"Jackson tells me you're having trouble finding a roofer," Ash said to Linc just as they were winding up for good-nights.

"The guy who was going to do it for me broke his leg," Linc confirmed.

"I've done some roofing. Between you and Jackson and me I think we could handle it."

"No kidding? That'd be great. It would save me losing two months or having to get somebody in from Cheyenne at double the expense."

While they went on to arrange a time to do the work, Kansas was thanking Beth for making her wedding dress, but Beth heard only a portion of either conversation as she stared at Ash in her second surprise of the day.

He was a roofer, too?

She was still having trouble believing it when they finally got around to saying good-night and went out to his car.

This time it was Beth who studied Ash as they headed for the ranch.

"Okay, who are you, and what have you done with Asher Blackwolf?"

He frowned at her as if she'd lost her mind. "What?"

"I was married to you for five years, remember? You didn't polish your own shoes, let alone make them for a horse. And I didn't think you knew which end of a hammer hit the nail. But here you are claiming you can roof the honky-tonk."

His frown turned into a slow, satisfied smile. "Did you think I was born in a three-piece suit?"

"Something like that."

"Well, I wasn't."

"So how come you always hired other people to do everything?"

"Because I was also fortunate enough to find myself in a position that afforded it, and hiring other people helped spread some of that around."

Of course that sounded like him. He'd put a number of Native American men and kids to work. And here she'd always just thought of him as too much of a desk jockey to dirty his hands.

Once again she was ashamed of herself.

"Where did these hidden skills come from?" she asked in a quiet voice that was the best she could do to convey her admiration of what he'd done while she'd been giving him less credit than he was due.

"Where else? My grandfathers."

"Your Grandfather Blackwolf was a sculptor," she reminded.

"He didn't start out there, though. He was a blacksmith and welder by trade before that."

"And he taught you?"

Ash nodded. "The Indian way is to pass things down. Stories, customs, skills. I knew my way around a forge and an acetylene torch by the time I was nine. But I preferred the construction work Pap did. Or maybe it was just that being around Pap was a better time," he added pointedly, tossing her a sidelong glance.

Since she'd already blown an apology for that earlier comment, she didn't think she ought to try a second. Instead she said, "I knew Robert worked in construction before he retired, but I didn't know you did, too."

"It paid my way through college."

For a moment Beth was lost in the image of Ash in completely different scenarios than she had ever pictured before. She was aware that his two grandfathers had shared in raising him after both his parents were killed in a drunk-driving accident when he was seven—his father having been the drunk driver, his mother the drunk passenger. Each of them had had serious alcohol problems. But he'd never said much else about his growing-up years.

"Amazing," she muttered to herself for the second time that day.

"What? That I can actually work with my hands and back, along with my brain?" he asked as if he expected another insult from her.

"No. That I could be married to you for five years and actually know so little about you."

He pulled up in front of the ranch house just then, but he left the motor running. Even so, Beth didn't move to get out and neither did he. Instead he turned toward her much the way he had when they'd begun the evening; this time, though, he stretched his arm across the back of the seat, close enough to her neck for her to feel the heat of him.

She looked up into the dark shadows of his eyes. "What else don't I know?"

He shrugged as if he weren't sure what to tell her.

"Were you a bed wetter? Did you suck your thumb until you were twelve? Were you an unruly teenager who got arrested a dozen times before you settled down? Did you lead a madcap college life? Do you knit?"

He laughed at her suggestions, and the deep, rich sound seeped in through her pores to sluice along her nerve endings like warm honey.

"I was not a bed wetter or a thumb sucker, but yes, I was a pretty bad teenager. I smoked and drank and gave my grandfathers fits. I never got arrested, but there were a few times that the cops brought me home or showed up on the doorstep. Either they were warning me to stop drag racing or they had a pretty good hunch I'd been a part of a bunch of kids who'd vandalized mailboxes in a drunken spree. And college—well, that started out as one big party, but by my senior year I cleaned up my act."

Beth blew a wry sigh and shook her head. "I can't even imagine you like that. Especially the drinking part. You rarely even have wine or a beer, and I've always thought that because of your parents' problem you had an aversion to it."

"More like because of my parents' weakness to booze, I was drawn to try it, too. I don't know. As a kid maybe drinking and being as wild as I'd heard they were was my way of feeling connected to them. It proved I was their son."

"What straightened you out?"

"Not what. Who. Pap. My other grandfather died just before the end of my junior year in college and I was about to inherit everything he had. I thought it meant life from then on was going to be one big party. Or one big drunken brawl, which was what the parties always turned into."

"So why didn't it mean that for you?"

"Pap kicked my butt, to be blunt. And then he met with the elders of the tribe—a number of men in key positions in the community who Pap happens to be close to—and they devised a plan for how I was going to spend my summer vacation that year."

"Not as a kids' camp counselor, I take it."

"Hardly. They managed to temporarily delay my getting my hands on any of the inheritance. I couldn't get a soul on the reservation to hire me, and Pap refused to let me live with him, turned his back on me completely. All of a sudden I was on the streets, literally, forced to sleep with the derelicts, eat at the soup kitchen, clean toilets at the bathhouse in exchange for an occasional shower. And more than once I was picked up by a cop friend of my grandfather's so I could get a firsthand look at a drunk driving accident or the corpse who came out of it."

Having lived on the reservation herself, Beth understood enough about the Native American community to believe this closing-of-ranks to scare one of their own and save him if they could.

"Sounds awful," she said. "But it turned you around?"

Ash nodded. "I really saw how tough life could be. And how easy I'd had it. It lit a fire under my conscience. Plus, having Pap turn his back on me was terrible. I knew it was only a matter of time before the inheritance had to be released to me, but I also knew that if I didn't stop drinking, he'd disown me for good."

"So you stopped."

"I did. Luckily I wasn't to the point yet where it was an addiction. And then I decided to do what I could with my other grandfather's money, to help out where I'd witnessed the need for that help. And that's how I turned into this boring guy you see before you."

Beth knew it was another reference to her earlier comment and this time she thought she'd better address it. "I didn't say you were boring—"

"Just no fun. And maybe you're right. You know what they say about all work and no play..."

But at that moment his overworking wasn't what was on her mind. It was still difficult for her to believe that she was hearing so much about him that she'd never known before. It was as if they'd just met.

"Amazing," she repeated.

"That I was once a wild man?"

"That you didn't tell me about it when we were married."

"Talking was not what we did best together," he reminded her, in a voice with a husky, sensuous intonation that alluded to what they *had* been good at.

But that Beth knew all too well. Their sexual attraction to each other had been so intense right from the start that apparently they'd skipped a lot of important aspects that normally happened early in a relationship—such as just plain getting to know each other.

"This earthier side of you—it's nice—for a change," she ventured.

Only one corner of his mouth tilted upward. "Is this Beth Heller trying to say there's something she might actually *like* about me?"

"It's just good to know what went into making you the man you are."

"Is it?" he asked, but in a way that made it seem more than an offhand comment. A way that seemed to wonder, just as she did, if there were more good things happening between them at that moment, for the air seemed charged with a new closeness that hadn't been there before.

A closeness that weakened her resistance to him.

His eyes were holding hers, searching them in the dimness of dashboard light, maybe for signs of what was going on here.

But he couldn't have found an answer, because Beth didn't know herself.

She knew only that she wanted more than anything for this man, who had just revealed such personal things to her, to close the gap between his arm and her shoulders, to pull her to him, to—

And then he did.

He leaned forward, wrapping his arm around her and bringing her to him so that he could cover her mouth with his in a kiss that held considerably more heat than the one they'd shared the previous night.

His lips parted over hers and his tongue traced the uneven edge of her teeth just before coming inside to play, to assert himself.

And Beth welcomed him. Welcomed the mingling of his breath with hers, the circling of their tongues, the thrust and parry.

His arm tightened around her, bringing her up against his chest, forcing her to circle the breadth of his shoulders with her own arms and giving her the opportunity to splay her hands against that hard back. Visions of those muscles working just beneath the taut, sweat-dampened skin she'd watched most of the afternoon danced through her mind and lit new sparks inside of her.

She had feelings for this man that she shouldn't have. That she didn't want to have.

And the longer that kiss went on, the more they sprang to life, until they scared her nearly to death and shoved her out of his embrace.

"I don't want this to happen!" she told him in a near panic.

And if she'd struck a blow earlier in the evening with her comment about his not being like Robert, she saw that she'd struck a much greater one with this.

Ash drew away as far as he could go, leaning his back against the door, taking his glorious arms with him.

"Then it won't," he said, in a tone she hated, for it told her he'd given his word and once he'd given his word, he didn't break it.

She closed her eyes and let her head fall against the window on her side as she fought the urge to make him take it back right then, to fling herself into his arms again and show him she didn't mean it.

But she did mean it.

She had to mean it.

She dropped her chin and opened her eyes to look at his again. "This is what we did when we met. We let ourselves get carried away and we never really got to know each other. So of course the marriage failed. But we're not married anymore. And the relationship we need to form now certainly can't be like this. If you're going to stick around—even for just a little while—we have to try to be friends, or at least courteous acquaintances, for the baby's sake. But we can't do this."

For a moment he just stared at her, and she thought that he really must have wanted to strangle her, because his eyes were so cold, so hard.

But then he nodded. "You're right."

"Good," she said, though she hadn't intended it to sound as halfhearted or as disappointed as it did, any more than she had intended to *feel* as disappointed as she did.

But once again she tamped down on it. "I have to go in."

He repeated his slow, solemn nod.

"Good night," she said, opening the door.

Once more his only response was the nod.

But she couldn't wonder about it, wonder what was going through his mind, wonder if he was mad at her because she'd stopped the kiss or mad at himself for starting it. She had to just get away from him before she began it all over again.

She closed the car door after herself and went up to the house, feeling his eyes boring into her as if they were laser beams. But she let herself in without so much as glancing back at him.

And once she was inside and the door closed her off from him, she fell against it as if the starch had gone out of her.

Hormones, she told herself. Crazy, intense hormones that was the reason tears were flooding her eyes.

It didn't have anything to do with Ash.

Or wishes that, somewhere along the way, things could have been different between them.

Chapter Five

Elk Creek's medical facility was across the street from the park square at the north end of town. Originally it had been the old Molner mansion—a three-level, red brick, Georgian-style building, its flat front interrupted by a big whitewashed porch.

The first floor was divided into a reception and waiting area, offices and examining rooms. The second floor was a small hospital, complete with two surgical suites for minor procedures and three rooms for inpatients, though it was rare that anyone stayed over. And the third floor held a lab, X-ray equipment and a rudimentary physical therapy section.

The entire staff was comprised of a doctor, a dentist—a coup for the small town—one nurse, one dental assistant, and Janet Gaultbien, who was receptionist, bookkeeper and administrator and just generally ran the whole shebang.

Beth's appointment with the doctor was at nine o'clock. She'd changed it since Ash had arrived and begun following her around, thinking that if she chose the earliest one, it would allow her to go before he showed up to tag along.

But Ash, Jackson and Linc were roofing the honky-tonk today and had begun at dawn, so she needn't have worried.

And as she climbed the porch steps, she wished she'd kept her afternoon appointment so she could be in bed still, catching up on the sleep she'd missed during the night. She promised herself that when she'd finished here she'd go home to her nice, air-conditioned house and take a nap.

That was what she was thinking about as she went in the front door, expecting to find the receptionist alone in the waiting room.

But the tall, boxy woman was not the only one there. Ash was, too, intent on a book Janet was showing him while she explained the development of the fetus at five months. Neither of them looked up.

"What are you doing here?" Beth blurted out, forgetting her vow to be nicer to her former husband.

He was leaning on the counter, his rear end jutting out at her from inside a pair of Jackson's oldest, rattiest jeans. His biceps bulged from the ragged armholes of a work shirt that had had sleeves once upon a time, before her brother had ripped them out, and he bore absolutely no resemblance to a businessman.

Her question drew Janet's attention, but it was a moment before Ash slowly straightened up and turned to look at her.

"I saw the note for your appointment on the calendar next to the phone in the kitchen yesterday. I didn't want to miss it."

"I think it's just wonderful to see a father-to-be so interested and supportive," Janet defended him.

And once again Beth felt like the bad guy. She tried to curb her tone of voice. "I thought you were busy roofing the honky-tonk today."

"We hoisted everything up and I showed Linc and Jackson how to get started. I'll go back as soon as we're finished here."

We? Well, terrific. Get this man into a set of stirrups on the double.

"When I wanted him around, he was too busy. Now I can't get away from him," she muttered to herself. Then, to him, she said, "I think we better talk about this."

"I'll tell Ramona you're here," Janet suggested tactfully.

When they were alone, Ash's eyes bored into her with the coldness that said he was angry with her. Already. "You know, it wouldn't hurt for you to be a hair less independent and let me help you with just one thing. For a change."

Beth reminded herself to be civil. "I know you're going to say something about our already having been intimate enough to get me here, but this is the first time I've seen this doctor and he'll want to do a full exam. And a pelvic is bad enough without an ex-husband as an audience. You can't come in. You've wasted your time being here."

His bushy brows drew together in a frown. "Actually, I hadn't planned to go in with you during the exam. I just wanted to be here with you. To be here *for* you," he answered through clenched teeth.

"Oh." Beth cleared her throat, again feeling chagrined.

He pointed his chin in the direction Janet had gone. "The receptionist said I could come in before and hear the heartbeat, but I won't even do that if it bothers you."

Great. He'd already discussed it with Janet. Janet, who thought his interest was wonderful. And who would turn around and repeat to the entire population of Elk Creek—by way of the small-town grapevine—either that, in spite of being divorced, they were acting like civilized adults and sharing this experience; or that Beth had turned her nose up at Ash's wanting to hear his baby's heartbeat.

Maybe coming back to Elk Creek hadn't been a good idea after all, Beth thought.

"Forget it," he said suddenly into the silence that she'd left while she thought about this. "I'll go back to work."

"No," she grumbled as he headed for the door. "I suppose I can stand for you to see my fat belly. But that's all."

He turned to her again, his gaze dropping to her middle as if he'd overlooked something before. But the bulge of her stomach was well concealed behind the oversize shirt she wore. "If it makes you uncomfortable—"

"It's all right." She didn't know if Janet had been secretly listening, but at that moment the receptionist reappeared to usher them both into one of the examining rooms without so much as questioning whether or not Ash would be allowed to go.

There was a bathroom connected to it and Beth was handed a gown and told to undress there while Ash was awarded a chair in which to wait for her.

She wasn't thrilled about going back into that room after she'd changed. A thin hospital gown with a single tie at the back of the neck was hardly a confidence booster. But she didn't have much choice.

Holding the gown closed behind her, she took a deep breath and tried to hide her real feelings about this, all the while wondering how she'd ever gotten herself into it.

The nurse was there by then and Beth was glad to see her, if only as a buffer between her and Ash.

Having Beth sit on the doctor's stool, Ramona took her blood pressure and pulse, finding both slightly elevated but accepting Beth's explanation of doctor's-visit nerves. Then she asked her to get on the table and lie down.

No mean feat, that. At least not while retaining her dignity and trying not to flash bare buns. But once Beth was there, Ramona helped out by covering her lower half with a paper sheet before pulling up the gown to reveal her stomach.

"Come on, Dad. You won't be able to hear from over there," the nurse urged.

Beth could feel her cheeks heat as Ash stepped to her side, standing just off her shoulder while Ramona squeezed a mound of jellylike ointment onto the small mesa of her naked middle. Then the nurse put an odd-looking stethoscope she called a Doptone into her own ears and slid the other end through the gel like a spatula spreading frosting until she found what she was searching for.

Beth and Ash both looked on as Ramona checked her watch, counting the beats before she held the business end of the stethoscope in place and handed Beth the binaurals. "Mom first."

Beth had heard the baby's heartbeat once before, at Cele's office, but it still gave her goose bumps as she listened while the nurse explained to Ash what it would sound like.

When Beth finally relinquished the device to him, he wasted no time bending low enough to fit the tips into his ears.

She could tell by his immediate frown that he wasn't sure he was hearing what he was supposed to. But as she watched, his eyes lit up and widened, his brows took flight nearly to his hairline and his lips parted.

And then, as she studied the pure wonder in his expression, Beth saw his eyes fill.

He caught up her left hand in his right, holding it tight and pulling it to press the back to his chest, just over his heart, in a gesture that joined their tiny family, that cherished her and their baby and brought hot tears to her own eyes.

And then she felt the baby skitter away, as if it had had enough of being eavesdropped on, and the moment passed.

Ash blinked the moisture out of his eyes, squeezed her hand one last time and let it go so he could pull the stethoscope out of his ears and give it back to the nurse.

But it was to Beth he said a quiet, sincere thank-you that made her rue ever thinking to refuse him this.

"I won't hang around," he told her then, as if giving a compromise of his own in appreciation. "Unless you want me to..."

She did want him to. She wanted him there with her—not through the pelvic exam—but to wait for the doctor, to talk about the baby, about hearing the heartbeat, about the nurse's guess that it was a boy.

But she couldn't bring herself to say it.

"You have a lot of work to do today. You'd better get back."

He nodded, just once, and if his smile seemed a little tight-lipped, she didn't understand why.

Then he left, along with the nurse, and she was alone in that room. Alone with the baby.

And wishing she wasn't.

Linc and Jackson were busy with the roofing when Ash got back to the honky-tonk. He climbed the ladder and pitched in without any of them saying much, and for the remainder of the morning that's how the time passed, leaving Ash free to think.

Hearing the baby's heartbeat had given him a new sense of connection to it. He could have stood there all day long listening to that tiny pulse beating its rapid rhythm through the rush of amniotic fluid.

And as he worked, it occurred to him that if he'd been loath to end that, how was he ever going to leave the baby behind once it was born? For even if he had custody half the time, that would still leave the other half the time that he'd be away from it.

But what was his alternative?

His mind wandered to one—if he and Beth got married again, he could take her and the baby back home....

But that idea was too farfetched to even consider. Beth could barely be civil to him. Even in front of the receptionist this morning, she'd nearly bitten his head off just for being there.

She'd mellowed, though...

Lying on that examining table, she'd let him take her hand. More than that, she'd held his in return, squeezed it back, hung on as if—for only a moment—she'd liked having him there.

He was probably just imagining it. Hadn't she basically shooed him away after that? Even when he'd offered to wait?

But there had been that moment, that one, brief moment, when they'd shared something very special. When they'd shared their baby. And that had been good.

Maybe good enough to build on . . .

Beth had a soft spot where the baby was concerned. No matter how tough she wanted him to think she was, how strong and resilient and capable of doing this on her own, the baby itself was her Achilles' heel. . . .

But her feelings for Ash didn't seem even lukewarm.

And there was no denying the problems they'd had in their marriage. Could they be overcome? Could he and Beth fix them and try again so they could be together in parenting this child? He honestly didn't know. But he had to explore the possibility.

For the baby's sake.

For his sake.

As a father.

And as a man who still had feelings for his ex-wife . . .

Did he have feelings for Beth? Maybe. But he didn't know what they were. One minute he wanted to wring her neck. The next he wanted to take her to bed.

How could remarrying her possibly be a good idea under those circumstances? Assuming he could even get Beth to consider the idea?

"Shall we break for lunch?" Linc suggested into his preoccupation.

Ash hadn't realized how late it was. Or how hot. "Sounds good to me," he agreed, all too willing to put aside what suddenly seemed like crazy ramblings.

He and Beth getting remarried? Maybe he was on the verge of sunstroke or heat prostration, because surely he was out of his mind to even consider such a thing.

Jackson put down his hammer, too, and they all headed for the ladder. Once on the ground, they went inside the honky-tonk long enough to douse themselves liberally with cool water, then met under the shade of a huge oak tree alongside the building to share the sandwiches Linc and Jackson had packed for the three of them.

"How'd the doctor's appointment go?" Linc asked.

"Fine. At least it went fine for as long as I was there. Beth didn't want me hanging around," Ash answered, watching a train come in at the station across the street.

"What's going on between the two of you, anyway?" Jackson demanded unceremoniously.

Ash glanced at him and then at Linc. "Should I be guarding my jaw?" he only half joked.

"I'm not sure," Linc answered, swiveling his gaze to his brother. "Are you askin' what his intentions are?"

"I guess I am. I caught Beth cryin' last night."

That took the humor out of Ash. "You must have needed to use the bathroom," he muttered, more to himself than to his former brother-in-law.

"I was just headed to bed after havin' a midnight snack. She had her back against the front door and big tears running down her face. I guess she didn't expect anyone else to be up, because she got plenty mad at me for catching her at it."

"That's Beth," Ash confirmed.

"Did you two fight after you left Kansas's place?" This from Linc.

"No, in fact, things went pretty well. For the most part. At least until the end."

"What'd you do then?" Jackson asked as if he were interrogating a criminal.

"Maybe you ought to mind your own business," Linc suggested.

Ash decided that confiding in her brothers might allow him some insight and answered Jackson anyway. "I kissed her."

Linc gave a hoot and a holler of a laugh. Jackson stayed as sober as Ash did.

"Guess she didn't want you to, huh?" Jackson said.

"Seemed like she did. Then all of a sudden she pushed me away and said she didn't. But she was dry-eyed when she got out of the car."

Linc chuckled. "When Virgie was pregnant with Danny she was like that. Crazy. One minute she'd be happy as a lark, the next I'd find her bawling her eyes out. It's hormones."

"You sure about that?" Jackson asked dubiously. "That doesn't sound like Beth. Beth's not a cryer. Shag fixed that when she was a just a little girl."

Linc looked at his older brother as if he were out of his mind. "Not even Shag could have kept a pregnant woman from crying."

Jackson stared at Ash directly again. "So what are you going to do about it?"

"Ha! I wish I knew" was Ash's only answer.

"Stay out of it," Linc told Jackson then, firmly this time.

"Just seems to me two people should be married when they're havin' a baby," Jackson said, as if he felt it his duty to get the words out.

But Ash didn't agree or disagree.

He was too lost in thought again.

Wondering what the hell it meant that his kiss had made Beth cry.

It was after dark by the time Beth heard Jackson, Linc and Ash come in the ranch house's back door. She was in her room working on the bridesmaid dress for Kansas's sister Della, and her first inclination was to rush downstairs.

She curbed it and just sat listening.

The house had been so deadly quiet all day and evening, and suddenly it was alive with the hum of deep masculine voices as her brothers and former husband apparently raided the refrigerator.

Then she heard them go outside again. She moved to the window where she saw Jackson slap steaks on the grill before he, Ash and Linc—now in swimming trunks—dived into the pool like three boys.

It felt good not to be alone anymore, even though she wasn't really with them. But when she analyzed the feeling, she knew it wasn't really her brothers' return she was glad for. It was Ash's. In spite of all her arguing against his hanging around, she'd missed him.

That was a terrible sign.

Since the air-conditioning was on in the house, her window was closed. She eased it open and propped a hip on the sill.

Tall, wrought-iron Victorian-style streetlamps surrounded the bricked patio but didn't cast much illumination on the pool, so she couldn't actually see them in the water. Rather than try, she closed her eyes, leaned against the window frame and merely listened, eager for the sound of Ash's voice joking and teasing her brothers as if he were a member of their close-knit club.

They weren't saying anything important. In fact they sounded slaphappy, no doubt from putting in a fifteen-hour day of backbreaking work in ninety-six-degree heat. But it was still good to hear. In fact, it made her smile.

Twice the ringing of a timer sounded to remind them to turn their steaks. They argued about who would get out of the water to do it, but both times Jackson did, grumbling about ruining good beefsteak. When the timer went off a third time, Beth opened her eyes and watched as they all got out, not bothering with towels, and disappeared from her view, no doubt to sit at one of several tables closer to the house to eat.

That they did in silence, making Beth smile again at the seriousness with which men attacked a steak. Or maybe they were all too tired to say anything, because their meal was over quickly, and once again Beth heard chairs scraping the brick. Both Linc and Jackson announced they had to get some sleep, inviting Ash to stay in the guest room.

Beth's pulse doubled, but she wasn't sure if it was from the thought that he might accept or that he might decline.

He declined. "Beth wouldn't be happy about that," she heard him say. "I'll just lie here and rest a minute and then I'll go back to the lodge."

She couldn't see him but assumed he'd moved to one of the loungers. And with the thickness in his voice as they all said good-night, she knew he was halfway asleep by the time her brothers came inside.

There'd be dishes to clear in the morning, because she didn't hear so much as a single plate hit the sink before her brothers climbed the steps, mumbled more good-nights and closed their bedroom doors behind them.

She could tell that Linc immediately threw himself on his bed and that was that. From Jackson's room there were sounds of him puttering around a little before his bedsprings squeaked and all grew quiet.

Then there was only silence in the house again.

And outside of it, too.

She didn't have to see Ash to know he was sound asleep down there, and for a moment she considered just letting him be. But she hated to see him spend the night in a lawn chair after the work he'd done to help her brother. She decided to go down and offer to drive him to the lodge so he could get some decent rest.

There was also the fact that she had an irresistible urge to see him, but she didn't want to think about that.

She was still dressed, wearing a pair of cutoff jeans that barely peeked out from beneath her sleeveless chambray shirt. Her feet were bare, but she didn't bother to put shoes on.

She padded noiselessly through the house as far as the sliding door in the kitchen that led to the patio. But instead of going out, she stood at the screen, studying Ash.

Just as she'd imagined, he was on one of the redwood loungers. But he wasn't exactly lying on it. It appeared that he'd sat on the end of it and just lain back, because his head was midway up the seat and his feet were still planted on the bricks of the patio.

It couldn't have been too comfortable, yet apparently he was so tired it didn't matter. He was out like a light, his arms crossed over his flat stomach and one big thigh drifting like a yardarm in a breeze.

And for some reason she couldn't have explained if her life depended on it, the sight touched her.

He really was putting a lot of effort into smoothing the waters here. With her. With her brothers. And what he was getting for it was hard work, her bad attitude, and a feeling that he should be grateful just to be allowed to hear his baby's heartbeat for a few moments.

Maybe he did deserve a night in the guest room. Even if it would be difficult for her to know he was right next door.

She finally went out to him, standing at the foot of the lounger, between his knees. Although this man had been her husband for five years, she suddenly felt it an invasion of his privacy to be watching him as he slept. She was also trying not to pay attention to his bulging biceps or his thick, muscular thighs and well-defined calves.

"Ash?" she said softly so as not to startle him. "Ash, wake up."

His forehead knitted in a frown, but he didn't open his eyes.

"Come on, you don't want to sleep out here. Come inside."

Still, his eyes remained closed, but the corners of his mouth quirked up in what could have been called a drunken grin, except that she doubted he'd been drinking. Then his long, thick lashes finally made a leisurely sweep to half-mast. "Is this an invitation?"

"To the guest room," she said, still quietly, as if she might wake someone else.

"Nah, that's all right. I know you don't want me here."

"It's okay."

"I'm gonna get going to the lodge. Soon as I can move."

"Maybe you are drunk," she muttered, referring to the slow motion of his words and the ridiculous smile on his face.

"Did somebody say I was?"

"You just seem so silly."

"Do you like it?"

She did. A little. For once Mr. Take-Care-of-Every-thing-and-Everyone couldn't even seem to take care of himself. But she wouldn't admit it. "Have you been drinking?"

"Water. Lots of it."

"So you're just tired."

"Haven't done this kind of work since I was a pup."

"Well, come on and put your old bones to bed upstairs."

He sighed. "I don't think I can move just yet."

Beth didn't want to touch him. Any physical contact between them would be like holding a match head to a hot burner. But she didn't think he could move on his own, either, so she held out her hands to him. "Come on, I'll help you up."

A loopy, one-sided smile curled his mouth and he raised his arms, clasping her hands in his. But the moment he did, his weakness disappeared, and he pulled her down gently on top of him—chest to chest, stomach to stomach. With his thighs still spread wide, she had no choice but to bend her knees and let her feet fly like flags in the air, making her contact with his lower regions all the more complete.

"Very funny," she said.

"I thought so."

She tried pushing herself away but his arms were crossed over her back, a hand on each hip, locking her to him. The best she could do was raise her head and shoulders slightly above his.

"So much for being weak and tired," she said, trying not to be too aware of the feel of him beneath her.

"I missed you today," he told her in a way that left her wondering if he was joking.

"You saw me this morning."

His smile stretched into a grin. "That was something, wasn't it?"

She had the urge to rest her cheek on his chest, to relax atop him, let herself ride the hard hills and valleys of his big body like water over rock, and talk about the wonders of what they'd created together.

But of course she couldn't do that.

The best she could do was agree. "Hearing the heartbeat is incredible."

"I think I did pretty well at this baby making. Gave him a strong heart."

Beth laughed. "What should I take issue with first? That you're so cocksure the baby is a boy? Or that you're taking all the credit?"

"Doesn't matter. They're both true," he goaded.

"Seems to me that you only contributed one ingredient. I'm doing the rest."

The sun had darkened his skin to a ruddiness that she could see even in the golden glow of lamplight, and it gave a sharper edge to his facial structure, which made her think suddenly of a warrior, especially when his features contorted into a mock menacing expression.

He covered the sides of her rib cage with his splayed fingers. "Don't make me tickle you into taking that back, woman," he threatened.

"Tickle me and you'll never see daylight again," she countered, squirming a little to try to escape.

Not a good idea. She felt the bulge inside his swimming suit rise against her.

"Come on, let's just get you set up in the guest room," she said, in a hurry to end this play before it led to anything more.

But Ash wasn't so inclined. He did a slight, speculative tickling of her sides. "Admit what a good job I did making this baby."

"It's me who's making this baby."

"You're asking for it," he warned, giving her another taste of what was to come.

She tried again to push herself out of his grasp but it was useless. He held tight.

"Last chance," he said. "Tell me what a good job I did."

"I might holler for help and get my brothers down here after you, but that's all you're hearing from me."

"Okay. You asked for it."

Beth hated to be tickled and he knew it. A devilish smile played on his lips again and those fingers began to torture her sides.

She couldn't help writhing and wriggling even as she tried to get free. But all she accomplished was to bring herself closer in contact with him. Her traitorous nipples kerneled and strained inside even the bigger sized bra she wore, until finally she shouted amidst her own miserable laughter, "Okay, okay, I give up."

He stopped tickling her, letting his hands follow the curve of her ribs instead, the tips of his fingers just barely brushing the sides of her breasts. "Tell me what a good job I did," he demanded in a voice grown husky since it had last been used.

Her arms were tiring and if he didn't let her go soon, she wasn't going to have any choice but to collapse completely on him. "You did a wonderful job," she deadpanned insincerely.

"Not heartfelt enough," he claimed, curling his fingers for a second assault.

But just as he did, the baby gave the biggest kick Beth had felt yet. A kick big enough and close enough to the outside of her stomach for even Ash to feel it.

He stopped short, staring up into her eyes with a sudden look of shock and alarm. "What was that?"

Beth laughed at him. "What do you think it was?"

"The baby?"

Then it happened again.

"Is it all right?" Ash demanded.

Beth laughed again. "You did know they kick, didn't you?"

"This soon?"

"Sooner. I was feeling it by the time I went to see Cele, but then it was only a fluttering and I just thought I had butterflies in my stomach or was hungry or something. It's only been what I'd call kicks for the past couple of weeks, but this is the first time it's been this hard. It must not like to be tickled, either."

But everything that had come before seemed lost on Ash. His bushy brows were beetled and he sat up, swinging Beth to his lap at the same time and beginning to place a hand on her stomach.

He didn't quite make it before apparently remembering that he didn't have the freedom.

"Can I feel it this way?"

"You can try, but there's no guarantee it'll happen again right now."

He placed his hand over the bulge of her middle as carefully as if she might break, staring down at it as he did.

There were all sorts of shoulds and shouldn'ts that went through Beth's mind, but she quieted them and let herself enjoy the moment.

It felt good to be there, perched across Ash's thighs, the heat of his body all around her, one of his long arms bracing her back, his big hand palming the mound his baby made as if it were a small basketball.

He was so intent, so serious, so awestruck. All the playfulness had gone out of him, and he waited motionlessly, soundlessly, as if he meant to hold that pose no matter how long it took for him to feel the baby kick again.

Then it did, but much farther to the side.

"It moved," she told him, redirecting his hand just in time for yet another kick, though this one was more like what she'd been feeling before, just a gentle thump.

"Does it hurt?" he asked, sounding concerned.

"No," she answered with yet another laugh, hearing the sensual timbre of her own voice.

Being so close to Ash, having him touch her with a certain amount of intimacy, was getting to her.

Her own hand still covered his where it rested over her stomach, and she was suddenly very aware of the texture of his skin, of the sharp bones of his knuckles beneath her palm, of what it felt like to be caressed by that hand—for he was caressing her.

Somewhere along the way he'd stopped just waiting for the baby to move again and begun to knead her middle much the way she'd known him to knead her breasts in times past.

He also wasn't watching his hand anymore. When she glanced up, she found him studying her face. His eyes were coal black and shaded by the shelf of his brows and she knew he wanted to kiss her again. That he wanted to do more than kiss her.

And she wanted him to. Lord help her. She wanted him to.

All on its own her chin tilted, her lips parted.

His gaze dropped to them. He moved slightly nearer. But then he stopped.

He'd given his word the night before that this wouldn't happen again. Beth knew he remembered it. And that he wouldn't break it.

But never in her life had she craved anything as much as she did the feel of his lips on hers at that moment. And she *hadn't* given her word.

Still holding his hand to her stomach, she reached with her free hand to the side of his face and raised herself enough to press her mouth to his as tentatively as if she'd never kissed anyone before. It flashed through her mind that if he rejected it, she had it coming for the two times she'd rejected him.

But he didn't.

His lips parted and he accepted the kiss, answered it with a patience that somehow seemed strained, as if he had to force himself not take over.

His arm around her back tightened. His hand at her middle kept up the caress her breasts yearned for, and his tongue followed her lead, but he initiated nothing, driving her all the wilder inside with wanting him.

Then he ended the kiss, slowly, gently, regretfully enough that it wasn't a rejection but more like a first-date kiss that had gone far enough.

"Your idea of getting to know each other without sex clouding it—the way we should have the first time around—was a good one. Let's work on it."

At that moment, with every nerve in her body awake and alive and desire already turning her skin sensitive, that seemed like the worst idea she'd ever had.

But she wasn't about to let Ash know that, so she merely nodded her agreement. And this time when she tried to get up, he let her go.

She glanced in the direction of the house. "It really is okay if you stay in the guest room," she lied, because wanting him the way she did at that moment made it less okay than it had been before.

He shook his head. "I wouldn't stay in the guest room. I'd last about ten minutes and then I'd be in your room."

Sounded good to her. Not that she'd say that, either. "Then let me drive you to the lodge."

"I wouldn't let you drive back out here alone last night, and I'm not going to tonight." He stood and her eyes rode his chest all the way.

"What if you fall asleep behind the wheel?"

"I won't. I'm wide-awake now."

She understood the feeling. Desire pumped adrenaline through her, too.

He cupped her chin between two fingers and tilted it as he bent low enough to kiss her once more, chastely, gently. "We have to finish the roof tomorrow, and Linc's bachelor party is in the evening, so I may not see you until the day after."

She laughed at that, though wryly. Hearing it sparked vivid memories. It seemed their entire marriage had been a series of similar statements—one job or engagement or expectation on top of another, all strung together to keep him busy elsewhere. And even though his absence was what she'd been telling herself she wanted, even though it was her brother he was helping, her brother's party he was going to, it felt bad.

Bad enough to remind her that there were things she needed not to forget.

"Sure," she said.

Her tone made him frown again, more seriously this time, but she didn't give him the chance to ask.

"Be careful driving back to town," she said, turning from him.

"Beth?"

She didn't pause. "Good night," she called as if he hadn't said anything, going into the house and locking the sliding door behind her.

Ash was still standing where she'd left him, watching her, his hands on his hips, his confusion obvious even from a distance.

But rather than let him know what was going on inside her, she gave him a small smile and a parade-pretty wave.

Then she went through the kitchen and up to her room, wishing all the way that the reminder had the power to keep her from wanting him with her so much she could cry.

Again.

Chapter Six

Beth spent the following day doing the final handwork on Della's bridesmaid dress for the wedding and listening intently for sounds of her brothers returning from roofing the honky-tonk. Try as she might, she couldn't help waiting anxiously, hoping they'd be done early and Ash would come home with them.

It didn't happen.

She delayed leaving for Kansas's house until Linc and Jackson returned, but Ash wasn't with them. He'd gone to the lodge to shower and change for the bachelor party.

It was good, she told herself as she drove to Kansas's place. Good that she'd had all day to feel the old loneliness, the old longing to see him. It was good that now she felt the old disappointment, the old sense of taking a back seat to other things he was doing; of being out of sight, out of mind.

It was all good, because it put things into perspective for her. Things it was easier for her to lose sight of when her view was filled with Ash.

Kansas's sister Della and her four kids were already there when Beth arrived. As was Danny, who had been staying with Kansas while Linc worked on the roof.

They ordered pizza and broke out a bottle of wine for their own small wedding-eve celebration, taking care of last-minute details while the kids all played outside.

Of course Beth didn't touch the wine, but she did enjoy the companionship and camaraderie of the two Daye sisters as the liquor loosened them up.

Della drank by far the most, and by the time she gathered her kids to walk home, she'd gone from being giddy to being sentimental.

"I'm glad you're marrying Linc," she told Kansas, as Beth stood by while the sisters hugged.

Kansas thanked Della and told her she loved her, then made a joke to lighten the moment before Della finally left.

"Let's get Danny to bed and then we can relax," Kansas suggested as they herded the little boy back inside.

Beth didn't do much in the way of putting her nephew down for the night. Kansas was already mothering the three-year-old and Danny seemed to have accepted her as just that—his mom.

Things would be good for Linc and Kansas and Danny, Beth realized, feeling a wave of sentimentality of her own. They might be a ready-made family, but they seemed to fit together as if it were meant to be. And, as she so often did, she envied them what they had together.

When Danny was in bed, Beth and Kansas took two glasses of ice tea and sat on the white wicker chairs on the front porch.

"So, how are things?" Kansas asked then, making it sound very much like a leading question.

"Good. Everything's good," Beth answered as if she hadn't understood her friend's intention.

"You know, Linc and Jackson are worried about you."

"I don't know why. There's no reason to be." Beth could feel Kansas watching her in the dim glow of the porch light, but she merely pretended a great interest in the railing.

"Is everything all right between you and Ash?"

How did a person answer a question like that under the circumstances? Beth shrugged. "He's still here" was all she could think to say.

"Is that good or bad?"

"It would be good if he left."

"Then it's bad that he's here," Kansas concluded.

"Well, not really bad, no," Beth hedged, for her conscience wouldn't allow her to make Ash the villain. The only thing bad about his being here had been her own difficulties controlling her feelings for him.

"Is it just that I had wine and you didn't, or is there another reason I'm confused?"

"Maybe because I am."

"Ah," Kansas said as if they'd hit on something. "Let me guess—you're still attracted to him, even though you're divorced."

Beth couldn't openly admit to that. Instead she said, "Ash is a good man. He really is. I admire and respect him."

"Umm-hmm," Kansas agreed with suppressed laughter just below the utterance.

"I always did enjoy his company—what I had of it," Beth conceded, feeling as if she were going a little further out on a limb and yet unable to stop herself. "He has a great sense of humor and he can be very attentive. He's generous and caring and sensitive..." Just remembering the sight of tears in his eyes as he'd listened to the baby's heartbeat the day before made her own eyes sting. "And I'm sure he'll be a good father," she added quietly.

"None of that makes him sound like someone you wouldn't want to have around. Does he repulse you physically or something?"

Beth laughed spontaneously and wryly at that, giving herself away. "Lord, I wish he did," she muttered.

"Then you *are* attracted to him."

Turned on by him. So hot for him she could melt—and very well might have the night before if he hadn't stopped things before they even got started. But she avoided responding to her friend's statement. "His being here is only an interlude. A brief interlude, I'm sure."

"And then what?"

"And then he'll leave. Like the last two days with the roofing, for example. Someone or something somewhere will need him—for a good reason, a good cause, in a way that I totally agree he should accommodate—and he'll be off again. His being here now, spending time together, isn't the reality of what life with him is like."

Kansas murmured knowingly. "Linc said that whenever he visited the reservation he barely saw Ash, that he never knew if it was because Ash was leaving the two of you alone to catch up or if it was always that way."

"It was always that way. Ash and I never saw much of each other. He was—is—a busy man. He's diligent and selfless when it comes to his foundation. And it's important work. That's part of what I respect and admire him for."

"Still, if the two of you were separated a lot—well, you know what I think about that. That was why I refused to marry Linc the first time he asked. It must have been awful for you, being married to someone you hardly ever saw."

"It wasn't good for either of us," Beth said, her voice sounding far away even to herself. In the back of her mind she was revisiting that awful moment when she'd announced she no longer wanted to be married to him and he'd so calmly, so matter-of-factly, agreed. "Although I have to admit I didn't know he was unhappy, too, until I told him I wanted a divorce." She was surprised to hear herself admit that out loud. "Up until then I thought he was okay with the way things were, that it was just me who the marriage wasn't working for."

"And it wasn't?"

"I guess not," Beth answered, hating that her voice cracked and she was unable to elaborate, even though it was obvious Kansas was waiting for her to. How could she explain something she didn't understand herself?

Instead she cleared her throat and went on as if she hadn't been bothered in the slightest. "So he moved into his grandfather's house by noon the same day we talked about it and that was that. Quick, clean and easy." Except that their divorce hadn't been any of those things, no matter how she'd been able to make it look then or sound now.

"Does that mean that even having the baby doesn't make you want to go back to him?"

"I wouldn't ever want to go back to the way things were before, no," she said sadly. Then, as Kansas had done with Della's parting emotionalism, she tried to lighten the tone. "If someone promised I could have what you and Linc have together, though, who knows?"

"Babies should have fathers in the home." Kansas seemed to think she was agreeing with something.

"Like I said, I'm sure Ash will be a good father anyway," Beth insisted, trying to keep up a positive attitude, although the image of her and Ash and the baby as a small family was achingly appealing. But what kind of lessons would her child learn if it was raised in a loveless marriage? "We were just lousy at being married," she added firmly, hearing the note in her own voice that said she needed to remember that.

Ash had arrived at the ranch long before Linc's bachelor party was set to start, in hopes of having a few minutes with Beth. But he hadn't known she was going to Kansas's house for the evening, and by the time he got there she was gone.

As the night wore on, it seemed more and more likely that he wouldn't see her at all today, and while he nursed a glass of soda water, sitting back from the rest of the guests, he wondered at his own feelings about being away from his former wife these past two days.

It was like old times—his being busy, their both going in different directions so that their paths barely crossed.

But unlike before, now it was bothering him.

And he wasn't sure why.

Probably, he decided, it had to do with the baby. With this sense he had of wanting to catch up on the five months he'd already lost.

And yet, as much as he didn't want to admit it, his mind wasn't really on the baby. It was on Beth.

And that made him begin to analyze his feelings for her.

Because he did still have feelings for her and he was kidding himself to deny it. He cared about her. And not just about her health and well-being because she was carrying his child. He cared about the woman herself.

Maybe more than he had in a long time.

And that realization shocked him.

The only explanation he could come up with, when he thought about it, was that for some reason marriage had buried those feelings.

Was it possible that after three years of being with a woman who kept every emotion under tight wraps, he'd closed himself off, too? That he'd hidden his own feelings even from himself?

Maybe it had been a protective mechanism, he thought as a cheer roared up in the room from a raunchy videotape someone had started in the VCR. Maybe after a long time of never hearing her tell him she loved him, of her never letting him know she felt anything for him at all, he'd locked up his feelings for her, too. Because even though he'd tried to convince himself she must care for him at least a little, the longer he'd gone without a sign, the more he'd begun to wonder. And the more he'd buried his own feelings just in case they really weren't reciprocated.

But he was seeing different things in her now, in spite of all her attempts to maintain her usual show of imperviousness. He'd actually seen tears in her eyes at the sound of the baby's heartbeat, and she'd held his hand—hard—and shared that moment with him as much as any loving wife might have. He'd seen regret that she'd insulted him by saying he wasn't like Robert. And there was a general softening to her, a new warmth that seemed to sneak out when she wasn't hiding it.

Could it just be related to the onslaught of those pregnancy hormones Linc had talked about? Or was it possible that she might still have feelings for him? In spite of all she'd done to push him away?

He hoped it wasn't only pregnancy hormones.

Because if he had to face that his own feelings for her might be lurking beneath the surface, close enough to find new life, he wanted to believe her feelings for him were in that same position.

A loud hoot called his attention to the big-screen TV, and he was glad to be drawn from these thoughts he couldn't be completely comfortable with.

But he didn't have a taste for the movie, and rather than join the group, he headed for the kitchen. He hadn't noticed that both Linc and Jackson had slipped away from the festivities, but there they both were, too.

"Need a fresh drink?" Jackson asked.

Ash handed over his glass and popped a few peanuts into his mouth. While he ate them, he craned around the two brothers for a look through the window at the garage. "Is Beth spending the night with Kansas?" he asked Linc, who was clearly feeling no pain as he leaned against a counter with a ridiculous grin on his face at nothing in particular.

But it was Jackson who answered. "Nah, she got home a few minutes ago. She was sneaking up the stairs when I came in here."

Ash had been trying to keep a pretty close eye on the front door so he'd know if she arrived, but clearly he'd been so lost in his own thoughts that she'd managed to slip past him.

"Hold off on refilling my glass," he said in a hurry just as Jackson was about to. "I think I'll go up and say good-night."

Linc began to chuckle at that but Jackson only shrugged and set the bottle of soda water back in the refrigerator.

"Hers is the second door on the left," Linc offered.

"Thanks." Ash went back into the living room, heading for the stairs. Leaving the cleaner air of the kitchen, he noticed for the first time that the celebratory cigars had left the rest of the house thick with smoke that drifted to the second level.

If he had his way, he thought as he took the steps two at a time, he'd pack up Beth right then and take her to the lodge with him, away from the smoke and noise and bawdy movies playing in her living room.

And alone with him for the night . . .

But of course, he wouldn't have his way, so he curbed the idea as he knocked on her bedroom door.

She must have seen enough of what was going on downstairs to be wary, because she called a cautious, "Who's there?"

"Just me," he answered, half wondering if she'd let him in or tell him to go away.

But then he heard the sound of her lock clicking back and she opened the door.

She wore a loose-fitting sundress that left her shoulders bare, and it shot through Ash's mind to press hot kisses to one and work his way across to the other.

He fought the urge just as he'd curbed his thoughts.

What he did do, though, was surprise her, by moving her out of the way so he could step inside and close the door behind him.

"The place is full of smoke. Don't let any more of it in here than there has to be," he said by way of explanation as he looked down into her wide blue eyes. Then he released her and crossed the room to the two large windows on the facing wall, opening them both. "I don't want you sleeping in it, either, so leave these open all night, even if it does waste the air-conditioning."

He waited for her to argue, to get mad at him for giving her orders, but it didn't happen.

Instead, in a congenial voice, she said, "The party seems like a success. Are you having a good time even though you don't know anyone but Linc and Jackson?"

"Sure. Elk Creek is a lot like the reservation—everybody's friendly," he answered as he turned from the windows, thinking that no matter how friendly the partiers downstairs, he'd rather be up here in this room with Beth. But he didn't say that.

She was standing in the middle of the room, her hands in the two front pockets of her dress, her feet bare, one perched atop the instep of the other. She looked fresh and beautiful, and something hard clamped his heart at the thought that she wasn't his anymore.

He told himself to leave the room and escape the feelings, but his desire to spend a little time with her was stronger. He crossed his arms over his chest to keep them from reaching for her, shifted his weight to one leg and searched for something to talk about.

The party—she'd asked about the party and his feeling like an outsider...

"Actually, I've been downstairs watching Linc get toasted into a stupor, and thinking that it isn't too far from some Indian purification rituals that prepare a man for marriage. So I don't feel too far from home."

She laughed lightly and he let the sound wash over him like cool spring water over sun-warmed skin.

"He's getting polluted, not purified," she amended.

"Before a wedding ceremony, some tribes give the groom a drink that makes him violently ill to purge and purify him. I don't know how Linc handles his liquor, but at the rate this is going, I'll be surprised if he doesn't get sick. Other tribes take the man into the sacred underground kiva, turn it into a sort of sauna and sweat the impurities out of him. With all the bodies, and the cigars burning, the living room is about twenty degrees hotter than it is up here—not quite a sauna but close."

"I see your point."

Ash glanced around the room, taking in the single bed without so much as a headboard, the tall bureau on which several pictures rested, the desk that was stark enough to have come from a military school, the small television he'd bought her the Christmas before. The single item that could be considered either feminine or pretty or anything more than purely functional was a cheval mirror in one corner.

"Was this your room as a kid?" he asked.

"This was it," she confirmed.

Glancing around again, he assumed she'd stripped the place now that she'd taken up residence in it again, and hadn't begun to redecorate yet. Not that he had anything on which to base that. He'd never seen the room before. When they'd come back here for the few visits they'd made during their marriage, Beth had always insisted they stay at the lodge, in spite of the fact that this house had plenty of room for guests. But her father had been alive then and this had been his house....

Samuel Heller. Shag.

Not a nice man.

He hadn't liked the fact that his daughter had married an Indian.

"Have you cleared your little-girl things out since you moved back or were they gone already?" Ash asked now.

She laughed again. "Little-girl things?"

"Ruffled bedspreads and curtains, a dollhouse, dolls, stuffed animals, a dressing table—those kinds of little-girl things."

She pointed to the mirror in the corner. "I bought that last week. With the exception of it and the TV you gave me, this is exactly the way my room was the whole time I lived here."

Ash could feel his eyes widening at the thought. "I know you were a tomboy, but—"

"I did have a rag doll my mother bought for me before she died, but you've seen that."

"And that's it?" He couldn't keep his surprise out of his voice.

"Shag wasn't big on toys, and especially not dolls or stuffed animals. He said he might have gotten stuck with a daughter, but he sure as hell wasn't having a prissy little miss in his house."

No, his late father-in-law had not been Ash's favorite person. He'd always resented the older man's intolerance toward him as a Native American. But Beth had never said much about what kind of a father he'd been, just that after her mother had died, she and her brothers had lost what "rounded his sharp edges." And though Ash had assumed Shag Heller hadn't been overly kind or loving, he hadn't known the details. Hearing some of them now did not endear the man to him.

"What did you get for gifts?" he asked, his curiosity roused.

Beth shrugged. "The same things Linc and Jackson got—a hunting rifle, a new saddle, new boots, fancy belt buckles, expensive cowboy hats, things like that. He was generous—he just wouldn't allow anything froufrou, as he called it, anything that would make me a sissy."

"But you were a little girl. Little girls are supposed to be sissies and have things that are froufrou."

"Not with Shag as their father. I had to be as tough as my brothers. Sometimes tougher, and if I let him see anything less—" she rolled her eyes "—I'd pay dearly for it."

"How?"

She laughed as if she found the reminiscence funny even though the reality hadn't been. "How? Let's see, double chores, worse chores or maybe I'd find myself sleeping in the barn for a month. One time he caught me crying over something—I was about ten and I don't even remember what I was bawling about. He sent me out in a torrential downpour to herd cows from one pasture to another, in the dark, late that night, by myself, knee-deep in mud and muck."

"Just for crying?"

"Especially for crying. Or letting him know how I felt about anything—he read that as a weakness. That time he said I was flooding his house and he didn't want to look at such a sorry, soggy sight, that I might as well be out where everything was already wet so I'd fit right in."

She was still smiling wryly, but Ash found nothing in what she'd said funny. "I can't imagine that."

"No, I can't imagine your grandfather doing something like that to a little kid, either. But Shag? Well, he was nothing like Robert." She shook her head. "He had an answer for everything. If we complained we were tired, he'd show us what tired was—he'd have us baling hay until our backs broke. Gripe that none of our friends had to milk cows by hand just to keep in practice, and instead of not using the machines for a day, we wouldn't get to use them for six months. Whine that just once we'd like to sleep in on a Saturday morning, and he'd have us up at four instead of five every day. Complain about anything, and he taught us a lesson for it. We learned to keep our mouths shut about whatever was going through our heads."

Or their hearts. "Maybe it's a good thing I didn't get to know your father any better than I did," Ash muttered through a tightness in his jaw muscles at the thought of someone treating *his* kids like that.

"He was a hard man," Beth agreed. "That's why I told you it wouldn't do any good for you to try overcoming his prejudice. But he was still my father, and there were good things that came from his being a taskmaster. Just think of what a sniveling woman I might be if it weren't for Shag."

Or maybe she wouldn't have to hide when she needed to cry, or get fighting mad at anyone who caught her at it, Ash thought.

But he didn't say it. He just wondered why he hadn't known these things about her before. Might understanding what made her do the things she did have helped him to be more accepting of them? Of her? Could it even have given him the chance to break down some of the walls her childhood had built?

"How come we never talked about this before?" he asked, moving to the bureau to look at the photographs there.

"I guess for the same reason we never talked much about your growing-up years as a welder and carpenter—we just plain never talked much."

He had the sense that she could have said more on that subject, but she didn't, and he didn't pursue it. He didn't know why she was being open with him now, but he was glad and didn't want to scare her away from more of it.

He took a picture from the bureau top and studied it. In it, Beth was eight or nine years old, covered in mud, holding an equally grimy piglet under one arm and displaying a blue ribbon in the other hand. The grin on her face was so big, so proud, it helped to dispel some of the harshness she'd just shown him of her childhood. It hadn't been all bad.

Or maybe not so much bad as tough. Or toughening.

"This is great," he said, smiling over the photograph.

She came up beside him to see which picture he was looking at. "Cheyenne Frontier Days. I was the fastest kid to catch and keep a greased pig. I even beat out my brothers."

Still holding the photograph, Ash glanced at the others. There were two of her mother—one just a portrait, the other of her feeding a baby he presumed to be Beth. There were pictures of Beth and Linc, of Beth and Jackson, of the three of them, of her graduation. "Why didn't you bring these with you when you moved in with me?" She hadn't brought anything besides clothes.

"It was your house," she said simply.

"We were married. That made it your house, too."

Again she shrugged. "It always just seemed like your house."

He stared at her, at her delicate profile and the shine of her dark hair, and realized in that moment just how little he really did know about her. "If you didn't feel comfortable there, why didn't you tell me? What did you think would happen? That I'd make you live in the garage until you could appreciate it?"

"It was your house," she repeated with emphasis. "You liked it and it was a perfectly nice place. What I felt about it wasn't a big deal."

But how many things had she felt and kept bottled up inside, he wondered, telling herself they were no big deal when they really were? Maybe, all together, they'd chipped away at their marriage, at their relationship, at her love for him.

"It's not important," she insisted, and he could see she was shying away from the subject, so he let it drop.

He replaced the picture on the bureau and then pointed an index finger at it. "I would have liked to have that picture in our home."

He knew there wasn't really anything for her to say to that and wasn't surprised when she didn't respond.

He leaned an elbow amidst the photographs and turned his full attention to her, wishing all over again that he could take her into his arms, that he could change the difficult parts of the way she'd been raised and put a little tenderness and understanding into those years, that he could comfort her for them, even belatedly.

But he only reached a fingertip to brush her hair back slightly from her face, just to be touching her in some way. "Is the baby kicking today?"

"It was quiet all day, but earlier tonight it seemed to be having a party of its own."

"Can I feel?"

She hesitated, and he knew why. They were alone behind closed doors and there was intimacy in the air all around them. There was the intimacy of the room, the intimacy of the insights she'd given him into her past and what made her tick, the intimacy of their bodies only inches apart. And somehow he knew she sensed that, as much as he wanted to feel the baby move, he wanted the intimacy of contact with her, too.

"It seems to have gone to sleep now," she finally said in a rush, as if she'd argued with herself about it and worried that if she didn't hurry with a denial she might surrender.

It was in his mind to do it anyway. To press his palm to her stomach. To circle her small shoulders with his other arm and pull her closer still, to kiss her properly, thoroughly, without holding back all he'd held back until now.

For the first time he began to wonder if the force with which she'd rejected his kisses was more because she *did* want him than because she didn't. Could it be her need to hide that fact that had made her so vehement?

It would certainly account for her responding one minute and shoving him away the next.

That thought strengthened his willpower and he kept his hands to himself. If she cared enough about him to hide it, she must care a lot. But he had to be cautious not to set off the mechanism that caused her to strike out to protect that hiding place.

And he wasn't exactly sure how to do that, except that it seemed better to heed the warning of her refusal to let him feel the baby kick, and let her come around in her own good time.

"I'd better get back downstairs," he said.

She nodded, but he could have sworn her agreement was reluctant, and he wondered if what flashed through her expression before she hid it could actually have been disappointment.

"Jackson and I have to finish the roof tomorrow, but I'll come out and get you for the wedding in the evening."

"I'm going over in the afternoon to help Kansas get ready. I'll just see you at the church."

"Okay," he said, though he envisioned spending the day without her and then losing her in the crowd of the wedding, too, if they didn't go together. None of it pleased him. Not any more than the thought of leaving her right then did, but he knew he had to.

He straightened away from her bureau and went to the door, not looking forward to rejoining the revelry down below. He hadn't realized Beth had followed him until he stepped into the hallway and turned to close the door.

But there she was, standing in the opening, looking soft and beautiful and just the slightest bit rounder with his baby.

His resolutions wavered and he couldn't resist reaching a hand to the bulge of her belly, after all—just for a split second when he said good-night, as if he were saying it to the baby at the same time.

But as his hand slipped away again, he nearly brushed her hand. Had she been about to cover his and hold it there the way she had the night before, or had she meant to stop him?

"Good night," she said, sounding slightly embarrassed and making him hope for the better of those two possibilities.

But then, from the party, he heard Linc calling his name, and the uncertainty in Beth's eyes reminded him to let well enough alone. For now, at any rate.

So he merely repeated his instructions to shut her door and keep her windows open against the smoke, and then he headed for the stairs.

He didn't go all the way down, though. He stopped at the second step, waiting until she closed and locked her door again.

Even after that was done, he hesitated, staring back at the hallway behind him, at all those closed doors down its long length. He couldn't help thinking about how difficult it must have been for a little girl growing up here. In a house without a mother and with a father who raised her not only to be a man, but to be a hardened one.

It made his heart hurt for her.

But it also made him wonder if there really was any hope of scratching the surface and finding her feelings for him ready to be rekindled.

Because now he knew just how tough that surface had had to be.

And yet, as he finally forced himself to go the rest of the way down those stairs, he knew he had to give it a try.

Chapter Seven

White candles wreathed in tiny baby's breath flowers and tied with satin ribbons provided the only light in Elk Creek's church the next evening. The flames cast an elegant, intimate glow within the high-ceilinged chapel. There were so many white roses and additional baby's breath all around the altar that when Beth let her vision blur, the candlelight might have been glittering on pristine snow.

But she didn't let her eyes blur for long as she sat in the first row. She needed to see clearly to be on the lookout.

The church was nearly full by the time she took her seat, and she hoped that anyone who noticed her frequent glances over her shoulder would think she was checking out the guests or watching for the bride.

But she'd been with Kansas most of the afternoon, had helped her dress and left her only moments before to have her picture taken.

No, much to her own dismay, she was looking for her former husband.

Most of the small town's residents had been invited, and with each look up the aisle, Beth saw more faces she knew—some she'd become reacquainted with since she'd been back, others she recognized from when she'd lived here as a girl.

Everyone who caught her eye smiled or waved a little and she returned them all, but among the crowd she didn't see Ash, and she felt conspicuously alone—the only person on the whole front bench while all the rest of the pews were close packed.

Even across the aisle, Kansas's brother-in-law was being kept company by his parents and sister so he wouldn't be by himself, even though Della was the matron of honor and all four of their kids were in the wedding.

Not that Beth knew for sure that Ash would sit with her.

But still...

Then, on what seemed like her hundredth glance back, she saw him.

He was dressed impeccably. He wore a dove gray suit, white shirt and a mauve silk tie she'd bought him for his last birthday. He looked wonderful, but no matter how often Beth saw him dressed like that, she never failed to think there was something about him in the more formal attire that seemed slightly incongruous.

It was his hair, she knew. Even though it was neatly pulled back into a tight ponytail at his nape, the jeans and T-shirts he'd been wearing lately seemed more in keeping with those renegade locks.

Still, to her, he was the best-looking man in the place, and her heartbeat kicked up a notch at the same moment the baby just plain kicked, as if it were glad its father was coming to be with them.

And he *was* coming to be with them.

Shunning the usher's aid, he'd scanned the church until he spotted her and then started down the aisle. He didn't seem to notice the heads he turned as he did; instead, his gaze was trained on Beth as if he were hungry for the sight.

And though it shouldn't have, it pleased her very much.

"I wasn't sure you were going to make it," she said in a hushed voice as he stepped in front of her to sit down, leaving her closest to the aisle.

"I worked until the last minute so I could get that roof finished," he explained, bending near and inadvertently giving her a whiff of his clean-smelling after-shave.

Then his dark gaze studied her, starting with her hair, in its usual side-parted, curly, bob style. His eyes slipped over her face to her dress—a black sand-washed silk that fell loosely to her hips, where it was cinched to form a slight bubble over the figure-skimming skirt that reached to just above her knees.

"You look terrific," he said when he was finished taking it all in.

"Thanks. So do you," she answered before even realizing she was going to return the compliment.

Music began to play from the choir loft just then, and Linc and Jackson stepped from a side door to position themselves as a procession of two flower girls—Della's daughters—and three tiny ring bearers—Danny, and Della's two sons—started things off.

Everyone in the church stood to watch them coming, all five children very serious about what they were doing, but still wandering a little if they saw someone they knew along the sides.

Next came Della, dressed in yellow and looking slightly teary-eyed already, but working at keeping a smile on her face.

And then the opening bars of the wedding march heralded Kansas.

Her hair was sprigged with flowers and she looked beautiful in the gown Beth had made. The bodice conformed to her body from the narrow waist all the way up the high collar and down her arms to her elbows. The satin skirt was floor-length and ended in a slight train in back, all of it edged in the lace that had been Ash's contribution.

Beth was proud of both her creations, and for once it seemed that the feminine hobby she'd initiated to spite her father so long ago had been worth the battles Shag had waged over her squandering her time sewing.

Linc had stepped to the corner of Beth's pew, eager to meet his bride. When Kansas reached him, she gave him her hand, and he took her up the flower-lined steps to where the minister waited for them.

It wasn't anything at all like Beth and Ash's wedding, but somehow Beth couldn't help thinking about their own ceremony as everyone sat down again and the service began.

Shag had been opposed to her marrying an Indian, as well as being appalled that she and Ash had known each other only a matter of weeks. He'd refused to even attend their wedding, so they'd decided to have a private ceremony with only Ash's grandfather, her brothers and a very few friends in attendance.

They'd held it in the backyard of Ash's house on the reservation, and while everyone had been dressed in church clothes, there hadn't been a fancy wedding gown or tuxedos. Beyond the bouquet she'd carried, the only flowers had been in the garden, which didn't really come to life until after she'd married him and spent some time on it.

Still, she'd been so in love with Ash that the trappings hadn't mattered. And as she sat there now, seeing her brother's feelings for Kansas in every line of his face, her clearest memory was of Ash looking at *her* that way, once upon a time, too.

How did they come from that to this? she wondered.

And though she was happy for her brother and Kansas, the sadness that washed through her with the thought was almost unbearable.

"This shindig isn't easy on you, is it?" Jackson asked when he'd insisted Beth share the first dance with him some time later.

The reception was in the church basement. There were food and drinks galore, a live band, and once everyone had made their way through the receiving line, the party began in earnest.

"It's a nice wedding. Beautiful," she answered, maintaining the smile she'd pasted on her face as soon as the ceremony ended.

But Jackson studied her in his quiet way, and she had the sense that while she may have fooled everyone else, she wasn't fooling him.

"Seems to me a wedding can't be high on the list of things a person would want to do right after gettin' divorced."

She knew he was itching to add something about it being especially distasteful when the person was pregnant with her ex-husband's baby. She appreciated his restraint. Still and all, she could see her brother was worried about her, and so she was honest with him. "I'm trying to think of it as any old party."

"How're you doin'?"

"Not good," she admitted under her breath.

"We could say you weren't feelin' well or were tired out and I'd drive you home."

For the first time that evening her smile was genuine. Beneath Jackson's gruff, no-nonsense exterior was an observant, sensitive man, and the concern in his offer was very sweet. Beth even considered taking him up on it.

But as he led her around the dance floor, she caught a glimpse of Ash sitting patiently at their table, and she knew a lie about being tired or sick would worry him unnecessarily.

Besides, as difficult as it was for her to be here, there was another part of her that didn't want to end the evening before she'd really gotten to spend any time with Ash.

"That's okay," she told Jackson. "I'll be fine."

Her brother followed her gaze all the way to her former husband and then looked down at her again. "Can't say I understand this."

Beth started to explain about a lie upsetting everyone, but Jackson stopped her. "I mean, I don't understand what the hell's going on between you and Ash. You're havin' a baby together, he's hankerin' after you and you're hankerin' after him—unless I miss my guess—but you just keep at this divorce thing."

The way he put that made her laugh. "Divorce isn't something you *keep at*, like training a stubborn quarter horse."

"Yours has that feel to me. And it just doesn't seem right when neither of you is happy about it. Ever think that maybe this divorce just didn't work out?"

Beth laughed again but had to admit to herself that her brother wasn't too far off the mark—so far, her divorce didn't seem like a great success. Not when she was still so attracted to Ash, not when she couldn't stop thinking about him, not when she craved being with him and had to fight her feelings with forced reminders that she wasn't supposed to be experiencing any of that anymore.

"I'm also thinkin' that you still have a tender spot for him," Jackson said as if he'd read her thoughts and found something she'd left out.

"That's what you think is it?" she asked without committing herself to anything.

But whether or not she admitted it, he'd hit close to home, and denying it didn't make it go away. Or apparently hide it either, if Jackson had seen it.

A tender spot . . .

Yes, she definitely had a tender spot for Ash.

What she wasn't sure of was if it was more than that.

Or how much more.

Or if she could deal with it.

"He's a good man, you know," Jackson said, just in case she might have overlooked it.

Beth glanced up at her brother from the corner of her eye. "That's a switch. You're the one who hit him in the jaw that first night," she reminded him.

"Only because I thought he wasn't intendin' to stand up to his responsibilities. But he is. I think he'd do right by you if you'd just let him."

"Are the two of you in cahoots or something?" she teased.

"Now don't get me wrong," he said, ignoring her joke. "You know that house is as much yours as it is mine, and I'm happy to have you and the baby with me. Hell, it can get damn lonely there all by myself sometimes. And I don't mind at all bein' as much of a daddy to this child as you want me to be. It's just that you don't seem happy with the way things are, Beth, and I'm wonderin' if you should rethink it."

As if she'd been thinking of anything *but* Ash and this situation lately.

But to rethink the divorce itself? That seemed downright crazy.

"There were good reasons for Ash and me to split up. It doesn't need to be reconsidered," she finally assured her brother.

But as the song ended both their dance and their conversation, she didn't feel as certain as she sounded.

In fact, the longer she was divorced from Ash, the more uncertain she felt. And confused.

And unhappy...

But as her brother led her back to their table, she held all those thoughts and feelings at bay.

After all, it could be the wedding had just gone to her head.

And then, too, there were those hormones....

The reception lasted well into the night, and even when all the guests had gone and all the gifts had been loaded into Jackson's truck, Beth still didn't feel as if she'd seen much of Ash.

They'd sat at the same table and danced twice, but the wedding was the first social occasion she'd attended since she'd come home to Elk Creek. And that meant that all the people she hadn't seen yet used the opportunity to say hello. To catch up. And—in not just a few instances—ask questions to satisfy their curiosity about the rumors around town that she was expecting.

She'd talked to more people than she could remember, but she and Ash could never manage even a few sentences before someone else interrupted.

So she didn't mind that there wasn't really room for her to ride home with Jackson, what with Danny stretched out sound asleep across the truck seat and gifts spilling over into the cab. Instead she and Ash said good-night to him, and to Della and her family, and stayed to close up the church basement by themselves.

"Who cleans this place?" Ash asked as they checked to make sure no one had left anything behind.

"The ladies' auxiliary will do it in the morning."

"Good. I was afraid you'd signed up for it."

Neither of them had found anything significant amidst the general debris that littered the hall, so they locked the delivery entrance, made their way to the front and turned off the lights that were controlled by a main panel near the door.

"Nice wedding," Ash commented as they stepped out into the cool summer night.

"Mmm," she agreed as she locked up behind them and then hid the key in a small box that gripped the door-jamb magnetically, out of sight of any but those who knew it was there.

"Did you enjoy yourself?" Ash asked.

"Sure. Did you?"

He didn't answer right away. His car was back at the lodge and they began walking in that direction before he said, "I did a lot of thinking during it."

"I wonder if anyone who's divorced sits through a wedding without thinking about the hopes and dreams they had when they stood in front of a minister themselves. And how they didn't pan out."

Ash had long since taken off his jacket and tie, rolled his sleeves to the elbows and unfastened his collar button. He carried the suit coat slung over his shoulder. When she glanced up at him, curious about his silence, she found him staring beyond the tops of the buildings they walked past, at the sky.

Finally, in a deep, quiet voice, he said, "It occurred to me as I sat there that our backgrounds weren't the only thing we didn't talk much about."

"I suppose that's true enough," she agreed airily, hoping to lighten what sounded like a serious subject he was launching.

"And the biggest thing we didn't delve into was why you wanted out of the marriage."

So much for keeping things light.

"All you said," he went on, "was that you just didn't want to be married to me anymore."

There was accusation in that but he was right. She hadn't explained herself. To give him reasons when she told him their marriage was over would have meant telling him how he'd hurt her, how lonely she'd been. So she hadn't said anything at all then, and she didn't now, either.

Ash continued anyway. "Part of it is my fault. I didn't push for reasons, because I assumed you'd realized you just didn't love me and I didn't want to hear that in words—even if I could have gotten you to say it outright. But as I listened to that wedding ceremony, I decided that it's time I stop assuming or guessing and know for sure."

That wasn't a direct question, just a statement of what he'd decided, so she danced around it. "It's late," she said. Late at night. Late for them...

Though she wasn't looking at him, she could feel the heat and intensity of his gaze on her.

"I won't push it now if you're tired. But we *are* going to talk about this," he warned.

She knew that tone of voice. It meant his tenacity had kicked in. The same tenacity that found funding for difficult projects, lawyers for impossible cases, solutions for insurmountable problems. He meant what he said. He wouldn't let this rest until he was satisfied.

Beth stopped walking and took off her high-heeled shoes. His hand snaked out to her bare arm to steady her and she tried to ignore how good the strength and warmth of it felt as she took the course of offense as the best form of defense. "You never told me why you wanted the divorce, either. Just that you'd been considering the same thing and maybe it was a good idea." And her own voice was unsteady with the harsh memory of that, and the anger and hurt it had caused her.

"We'll get around to talking about that, too," he assured her. "But you're the one who initiated the split, so you can tell me why first."

They'd reached the lodge by then, a semicircle of ten small cabins built around a centrally positioned office. Ash took his key from his pants pocket and opened the heavy wooden door to his cabin. "My car keys are inside. Do you want to come in and talk or shall I get them and take you home and we'll wait until tomorrow?"

She'd rather not have discussed this at all. "Are those my only two options? Right this minute or tomorrow?"

"That's it."

Beth sighed impatiently to let him know just how much she didn't appreciate this. But when she weighed the choices he'd given her, she decided the late hour now could work to her advantage by at least keeping the discussion brief.

She stepped into the cabin. "I'm not sure what you want to hear."

The close space was lit only by a chain lamp hanging over a small table to the left of the entrance. The air smelled of his after-shave, his soap, him. It was difficult for her not to be carried away by that and by being in a dim room alone with him and a bed that looked much too inviting.

Not wanting to get too comfortable, she put her shoes back on and perched atop the table. Letting her feet dangle, she clamped the edge with both hands in a white-knuckled grip.

Ash tossed his jacket across the back of one of the two chairs she'd ignored. Then he planted a foot on the seat, a forearm on his raised thigh, and met her eyes on an almost equal level, crowding her a bit as he made it clear they were about to get down to business. "I want to know why you divorced me."

She shrugged. "It wasn't a good marriage," she answered simply, as if that said it all.

"We didn't fight. I didn't drink or abuse you or cheat . . . did you?"

"Cheat? You know I didn't or you wouldn't have come here so sure the baby was yours."

"Okay. That's true. I didn't really think there was someone else, though that would at least be something concrete to explain why you wanted the divorce. So what made it a bad marriage for you?"

She hated this. She absolutely hated it. There was no way she could talk about her feelings and not hate it. "It wasn't that it was a *bad* marriage. It just wasn't much of a marriage at all."

"It didn't live up to those hopes and dreams you mentioned earlier?"

"Actually what it didn't live up to were my expectations. Not that I had a whole slew of them. My mother died when I was so young that I never had much of an up-close example of what marriage was supposed to be. But the one thing I did think was that we'd be together. At least some of the time. And we weren't," she said flatly, as if there hadn't been any emotion involved then or now. As if, like two bottles bobbing separately in the same sea, they'd just drifted calmly apart. No big deal.

Ash breathed out a short, mirthless laugh. "You know, my grandfather made a remark about my being away from you too much. Does he know something I don't?"

She shrugged again, only this time it felt so stiff she had to force her shoulders back down again. "I think there just isn't enough of you to go around. Your work with the foundation is time-consuming. But it's also important, so it has to take priority. What's left over isn't enough to maintain a marriage, too," she said as if she could accept the reality without a problem.

Ash's bushy brows dipped together in a frown. "Are you telling me that you felt neglected?" he asked as if he couldn't believe it.

Beth didn't like the word *neglected.* Not at all. To her way of thinking, it made her sound weak and needy. And her tone toughened in response. "It was just very frustrating to compete with your work, with the foundation, and with the demands of a whole nation of Native

Americans," she finished with a flourish of exaggeration.

"You felt like you were in competition with all of that?"

"I *was* in competition with all of that."

"No, you weren't."

"Oh, come on," she said with a roll of her eyes.

"You weren't. The foundation is work. You were my *wife*. Two completely different things."

"Please."

"You weren't competing with it," he insisted.

"Okay. I wasn't competing with it, because I chose not to compete. Because I just stayed in the background and let it have you. Until I decided I didn't want my whole life spent in the background while everything else took priority over me. That's when I suggested the divorce."

He looked stunned. He sounded stunned. "Without so much as telling me you felt like this first? Without giving me a clue? My God, Beth, you always acted as if you couldn't care less how much my work kept me away, as if you were busy and wouldn't even know I was gone. Sometimes I had the feeling you were glad to be rid of me. Why didn't you *tell* me this?"

"What should I have said? I'd like to go to the movies tonight so don't spend the time to find a family that will take in the fourteen-year-old unwed mother, or an Indian home for that baby suffering fetal alcohol syndrome? Don't raise money for the homeless?" she asked wryly.

"How about just saying you'd like it if I was around more? If I could rearrange things so we could see each other?"

"As if I couldn't live without you? As if I depended on you?" she demanded, appalled.

"As if you loved me and wanted to be with me. And maybe even needed me just a little."

Her spine straightened reflexively. "I do all right on my own."

"Sure you do. At least that's how you always made it seem. You encouraged me to spend all the time I needed to at the office. To go to every meeting. To see to all the details of everything that came up. To travel when I needed to. You didn't mind. You said you had paperwork of your own. Or you'd go to the movies with my grandfather. No problem. Except that you damn well divorced me because I believed it and did do it all."

He looked as if he wanted to shake her.

"Would you have liked it better if I'd whined that we didn't see each other enough? Or begged you not to do what someone else depended on you for? Or pouted when a business trip took five days instead of three?"

"There's a difference between whining, begging or pouting, and just letting me know you want me around."

But the difference was too subtle for her to see. "It should have gone without saying that two people who were married to each other actually spent time together."

"Not when you were pushing me out the door most of the time."

"Oh, please. As if I invented all the things that called you away or needed your attention. I was just being supportive in the face of the inevitable."

"Supportive?" His voice had risen, apparently with the level of his disbelief, and he actually laughed.

Beth didn't know what he found funny.

"Hell, all that support made me think you could only stand me around in small doses."

"Sure. I didn't want to be with you, so I worked on your causes and joined your groups just to catch a glimpse of you, or kept bending over backward to lure you home when I didn't think it would do any harm to what you were doing somewhere else."

He pointed a long index finger at her and said, "Boat!" as if it had just occurred to him that that was the purpose of the game.

"Yes, Boat," she said, embarrassed to have admitted even that much.

He sighed and shook his head. The anger of moments before seemed to have evaporated, along with his need to discuss the reason for the divorce, as more pleasant memories took over. "Boat was one of the few times I honestly knew you wanted me. You'll never know how much that meant."

"You stopped coming home even for that," she said quietly, suffering anew the rejection she'd felt at the time.

He laughed wryly. "That's because I started to worry that it was only my services in bed that you were interested in." Again he sighed away the tension in the room. "Some of the best memories I have are of Boat," he said, his voice a deeper, huskier timbre, lost suddenly in the past. "Remember the rainstorm last year?"

Oh, she remembered all right. It sent shivers along the surface of her skin just thinking about it. "It's a wonder we didn't catch pneumonia." She pretended to chastise him for what had really been a delicious addition to the game. "Opening all the windows so the rain and wind could come in, as if we really were out in a storm at sea."

"Making wild, abandoned love to match it," he reminisced in a near whisper that brought him close enough for her to feel the warmth of his breath against her cheek.

He shook his head and laughed yet again. "The marriage wasn't all bad."

She ignored that tie-in to what they'd been talking about, glad for any distraction from the more serious subject of before. "That was the coldest rain..." But even as she tried to make it sound bad, her tone gave her away.

"God, that was a great night," he said, with a groan that matched some he'd made in the act. "If ever there was a time I thought you might get pregnant even using birth control, it was that night."

"We *weren't* using birth control after a while. We ran out, and even that didn't stop things."

"There aren't any drugstores on boats cast asea in a storm. And as I recall we couldn't help ourselves."

"Carried away like two hormonal teenagers." The intended rebuke sounded more like a sweet remembrance.

He leaned forward, his beautifully boned face just inches from hers. "You needed me to keep you warm." He placed a brief peck of a kiss on her lips.

"I needed you to shut the windows."

"That's not what you said at the time," he reminded with a smug grin before he kissed her again, holding it a moment longer this time.

"I expected icicles to grow from my ears."

He moved just enough to gently bite one lobe and then pressed slow kisses down the side of her neck to the spot where it dipped to her shoulder. "I'd never have let that happen. But I do remember some pretty great goose bumps." He laughed. "Yeah—like those. I didn't know you could do it on demand."

The goose bumps were hardly voluntary. They came in response to his kisses.

At any rate, her resistance was low, and so the sparks he rained through her went unchecked. The best she could manage was another phony complaint about that earlier event. "Not to mention that the neighbors could probably see what we were doing, since the curtains were open to let in the weather."

"The electricity was out and there wasn't even a moon." He reached behind her and turned off the wall switch so his room—like theirs that night—was lit only by milky light from outside.

He laid his palm against her cheek. "What a night that was," he said again, just before covering her mouth with his, completely, firmly, insistently.

His lips were parted and he urged hers open, too. Not that it took much persuasion. Beth let her head fall back and answered his kiss, the parting of his lips, even the first meeting of his tongue and hers.

He still smelled faintly of after-shave, and she breathed deeply of it, enjoying it, for once savoring what it did to her senses instead of fighting it.

On its own, one of her hands reached inside his collar to the side of his neck, thick and corded and strong. His skin was smooth, warm, and she had much too vivid a memory of what it had felt like to have the whole length of his naked body against hers.

She raised her other hand to his chest, telling herself to push him away. But that wasn't what she did. Instead she just left it there, wishing in her heart of hearts that his shirt wasn't between them.

His kiss turned more insistent, as if answering the need she felt. Her back arched her closer to him.

He helped that along by wrapping an arm around her, pulling her more to the edge of the table where her knees just brushed the hard ridge of his desire for her.

Aware of that, she told herself to stop this. Now.

But she didn't pay much attention. Too many wonderful things were awake inside of her, awake and crying out for Ash.

She felt his hand slide from its caress of her cheek to her back. Slowly, slowly, he pulled her zipper down, and as he pulled it, her dress inched lower on her breast, stopping tantalizingly near the hardened crest.

She meant to stop him. She really did. But her body, her breast ached for his touch, cried out to know the feel of his hand against her, and rather than moving away from him, she arched even more seductively toward him.

His mouth left hers, nibbling, kissing, following the curve of her throat, the hollow, with his tongue.

And then he very carefully covered her breast with his hand.

It felt good. Great. Terrific. But, oh, how she wanted that dress out from between them!

She rolled her shoulder so it would fall further. Or maybe so he'd realize that if he didn't push down that silky fabric soon, she might go crazy.

He chuckled, a soft, barrel-deep sound from inside his chest, but he got the message, because he slipped the dress lower and finally, gloriously, bared her breast to the air, then to his palm.

Incredible. The feeling was like nothing she'd ever known before. Never in her life had she reached the level of sensation she did then.

"You are bigger," he whispered, as if confirming her need for those larger bras he'd pretended not to watch her buy, and for the first time she found pleasure in what before had only been a nuisance. She was bigger. And better. Much, much better...

As if he sensed that every touch, every caress, every kneading of her flesh was intensified a hundredfold, he explored this change slowly, tenderly, carefully. Almost too carefully, for she craved the touch she'd known from him before—firm, strong, possessive.

But more than that she yearned for his mouth there, covering that engorged crest, nibbling, teasing, tormenting as only he could...

She slipped her arms over his shoulders and buried her face in the side of his neck, kissing him, teasing him, urging him to go further.

But he didn't, and the frustration it raised in her began to remind her of the frustrations she'd felt when they were married, those same frustrations he'd just moments before insisted she tell him about.

And in the instant of that thought, and the flood of unpleasant memories it brought with it, she heard what almost sounded like her father's voice echoing through her mind, telling her that only idiots were slaves to their emotions and that they always paid dearly for letting anyone see the weakness those emotions caused.

She recoiled from Ash, sliding her dress back between her breast and his hand.

"This is Linc and Kansas's wedding night, you know, not ours," she said, trying to make a joke out of the abrupt ending she'd put to what was happening between them.

But it didn't come out sounding humorous, and from Ash's raised eyebrow and tone of voice, he hadn't taken it that way, either. "I didn't think it was."

She seized a better excuse, the one she'd already used tonight. "It's late."

"Too late?"

She knew he wasn't asking about the time. He was asking if it was too late for them. And in that moment she didn't know if it was too late for them or not. So all she said was, "It's been a long day and I need to get home."

"You don't *need* to," he challenged, as if to get an answer out of her that way. "You could stay here." He nodded in the direction of the bed.

Tempting. It was much, much too tempting. But the cooler her ardor got, the more vivid was the memory of so many other frustrations and unmet needs that had pushed her to divorce him in the first place, and she knew she couldn't give in to that temptation.

"No, I can't," she said, both in answer to his suggestion that she stay and as an order to herself.

Ash's black eyes searched hers in the moonlight for a moment before his hands came to cup the sides of her face. "Tell me what you're feeling," he demanded, sounding almost angry.

"Frustrated," she answered the same way. "Just like I felt when we were married."

For a moment he continued to stare down at her from behind a fierce frown, but then his expression eased and he actually laughed, though there was only irony in the sound of it. "Damn it, Beth, that's not what I wanted to hear."

What had he wanted to hear? That maybe she still loved him? That she definitely still wanted him? That any of it made a difference to the way things were between them? Because it didn't.

"I need to go home," she said, pulling out of his grip. "Are you going to drive me or shall I walk?"

He stared off over his shoulder at nothing in particular and then looked back at her and sighed in what sounded like no small amount of frustration of his own.

"I'm not going to let you walk all the way out to the ranch."

She slid sideways on the table until she was clear of him and could get down. "Then let's go."

He didn't follow her immediately. He left her waiting in the doorway while he stayed where he was, shaking his head again as if to say *I give up.*

And something inside of her cried out for him not to. Not to give up on her. Even as she stood there ramrod-straight, in control once again, and every inch Shag Heller's daughter.

Finally he grabbed his car keys from the bureau top and joined her at the door, holding it for her to go out ahead of him.

Neither of them said anything on the ride to the ranch. Once they arrived there, Ash walked her up to the house in spite of her insistence that he didn't need to.

Beth unlocked the door and opened it, but before she could step inside he took her by the shoulders, turned her to face him and kissed her again, soundly, firmly, passionately.

Then he let her go so abruptly she rocked on her heels.

"It isn't too late," he said then. "Not when I want you so much it hurts. Not when you want me. But maybe if you could just admit it—to us both—that might be the first step." He finished with a gentle jab of his index finger against her collarbone.

A first step toward what? she wanted to ask.

But she didn't.

Instead she said nothing at all.

He turned and left then, as if to stay one moment more might cost him the control of the passion that had resurfaced in his kiss.

And as Beth watched him go, she couldn't help wishing he wasn't leaving her. Wishing he'd kept her in that cabin, taken her to his bed, made love to her all night long.

But even as she wished it, she hated herself for the weakness she thought it shouted of.

Chapter Eight

The next day was the Fourth of July, a holiday Elk Creek celebrated with gusto.

Beth helped Jackson with a few minor chores that morning to speed things up. Then she took a quick shower, pulled her hair into a curly topknot at her crown, applied a slight dusting of blush and some mascara, and got dressed.

Her choices of what still fit seemed to be getting fewer every day, but she finally settled on a navy blue trapeze sundress with a tanklike top. There were twenty tiny buttons down the front and, in a burst of daring, she left the top three unfastened, showing a hint of her new cleavage that would no doubt scandalize Elk Creek. And tantalize Ash, though she pretended that had nothing to do with it.

She'd made no plans with him but still expected to find him waiting by the time she went downstairs, certain that he'd show up to insure they attend the festivities together. But only Jackson and an excited Danny were in the kitchen when she got there.

Not for the life of her would she let her brother see her disappointment, so she hurried them out the door as if she didn't feel they were missing one vital member of the party.

They took Jackson's truck into town, her nephew sitting on her lap on the high bench seat. But Beth was barely aware of the little boy's fidgeting. Instead it was Ash she was thinking about.

She told herself he'd probably figured on meeting up with her in town, but still it was in the back of her mind that something might have finally called him away.

It was bound to happen and she knew it. She'd wished for it.

But just the thought that today might be the day twisted her heart into a knot and made her realize that she didn't want him to leave.

Lord help her.

The truth was, she woke up every morning anxious to see him—in spite of all her claims to the contrary—and went to bed every night consoling herself in her lonely bed with the thought that she'd be with him again the next day. And only when they were together did she feel content, happy, complete....

Riding along in her brother's truck, she closed her eyes as if to block out what she knew that meant. The same thing it had meant the first time she'd ever had those same feelings.

It meant that she really did love him.

Still.

Again.

Whether she wanted to or not.

And she didn't want to, because it didn't change anything.

Sure, being married to him would have been good if it had been the way things were now, the way they had been since he'd come to Elk Creek—seeing each other every day, spending time together, getting to know each other.

But that wasn't the way it used to be. It wasn't the way it would be forever. This was just a blip in the reality of life with him. A blip that could right itself and be back on course any minute. And she'd best not forget it.

She opened her eyes and stared past Danny's at Elk Creek as they drove into it, lecturing herself that these were only feelings. And Shag had taught her well that feelings could be ignored. That they never needed to be acted on.

And if Ash wasn't here anymore?

It would be just fine. For the best, actually. And she'd deal with it. She wouldn't let it devastate her. She just wouldn't...

Jackson found a parking spot in the school lot and they walked the three blocks farther to the town square. The street around it was closed off to traffic so booths could be set up to sell food and crafts, and offer diversions like shooting galleries and a number of games of skill and chance.

The park itself was turned over to picnickers, while the pavilion in the center of it was the site of contests in pie eating, arm wrestling, singing, dancing, cake baking, hog calling, and a half-dozen events designed for the kids of the community to compete in. This year there were even a few carnival rides brought in to operate beside the courthouse to keep everyone busy until after dark when the fireworks display would fill the sky.

The first order of business was to claim a spot in the park and that was where Beth and Jackson headed, Danny riding on Jackson's shoulders.

Somewhere between only partially buttoning her dress and reaching Elk Creek, the stuffing had gone out of Beth's anticipation for the day, but she put a good face on it as they worked their way through friends and neighbors eager to say hello.

And then she spotted Ash.

He was standing beneath a huge old elm tree waving and shouting to them.

Run! Run the other way! that voice of caution shouted in her mind.

And her feet were moving, all right.

But not away from Ash—to him, as her spirits rose again and all of those dark thoughts lost their hold on her.

"You must have been here at dawn to get this place," she said when she, Jackson and Danny joined him. He'd spread a large blanket in the armlike roots of the tree that would shade them during the day but still leave them a clear view of the fireworks in the opposite direction that night.

"I didn't want you getting too much sun," he explained, shrugging off what had to have been hours of waiting for her.

His pampering was one more thing she knew she shouldn't allow. Her father would have considered it fostering weakness, and while she agreed that it would be a mistake to become accustomed to it, she couldn't help being pleased by it.

It would eventually end anyway, she reasoned. Just like this time they were having together. But what if, for this one day, she indulged? What if she turned off the negative voice in her mind and let go a little? It was a holiday, after all, and what harm could it do if, for such a short time, she reveled in Ash's company? In his attentiveness? In Ash himself?

Maybe all these mood swings had made her a little light-headed and frivolous, but she decided that the future would take care of keeping them apart. And even though she'd have to deal with the disappointment and the hurt and the myriad of other harsh emotions that would come with his leaving, at least she'd have this time.

Besides, it was already too late to think she could avoid any of those bad feelings—she'd felt enough of them on the ride into town at only the thought that he might be gone. They were just waiting to rise again when he finally left, no matter what she did or didn't do. So why not make the best of what she had for the moment?

Jackson set their picnic cooler on Ash's blanket and then glanced in the direction from which Rick Meyers, the Heller Lumber foreman, was calling his name. He waved at the tall redhead but turned to Beth rather than immediately accepting the other man's invitation to watch an amateur boxing match in a ring just beyond the booths.

"I'll take Danny," he offered.

"That's okay," Beth declined. "He wants to go on the carnival rides. We'll take him there." She finished with a glance at Ash. "You don't mind, do you?"

He was wearing those faded, low-slung blue jeans and a red T-shirt with a few of his buttons undone, too, exposing the arrowhead that hung around his neck. The shirt had long sleeves and, in answer to her question, he pushed them up above his elbows as if he were about to dig in to work. Then he held out his hand to the three-year-old. "I've been itching to get on those rides my-self."

Danny took his hand without hesitation, having apparently warmed up to him while Ash worked with Linc at the honky-tonk, and that settled that. The three of them headed off in one direction while Jackson went in the other.

If Danny missed his dad and Kansas as the day went on, he hid it well. In fact, he seemed to have developed a fondness for Ash that bordered on hero worship. It was Ash he chose to take him on the Ferris wheel, and Ash he looked to for advice about whether or not to venture a ride on the children's roller coaster.

And when one of Kansas's nephews made a derisive comment about Ash's long hair, Danny set him straight, announcing with a full measure of awe and pride in his voice that Ash was a real live *In'ian*.

They met Jackson back at the park for supper as the sun finally began to relent and drift behind the Rocky Mountains, but it was hardly a peaceful meal, as a number of Elk Creek's single women kept happening by to say hello to Jackson.

"I never realized how popular you are with the ladies," Beth teased, unable to resist.

"Only with the ones lookin' for a husband," he said, as if they didn't count.

"I didn't know you were a confirmed bachelor."

"I'm not. Just not interested in faces I've been looking at since I was born. It'd be like marryin' you," he told her. "I know every little thing about 'em. It's boring as hell."

"Oh, come on," she cajoled, nodding at what looked to be the third return of one woman, whom Jackson had dated in high school. "I'll bet you don't give them a chance to surprise you."

Jackson caught sight of Suzy Teaton making her way toward them again and seemed to suddenly have had his fill. Though whether of food or aggressive women, Beth couldn't be sure.

He wiped his mouth on his napkin, tossed the remnants of his meal into a grocery sack they were using for trash and got to his feet in a hurry.

But before he left, he bent down to Beth. "How about I give 'em a chance to surprise *you* and remind 'em all that I'm not the only available man sittin' on this blanket?" he goaded back as he took off in the direction least laden with admiring females.

Beth glanced at Ash to find a Cheshire-cat grin on his face.

"Want an introduction?" she challenged with a nod toward the now-retreating blonde. But she wasn't feeling quite as unaffected as she wanted him to believe. In truth, with the exception of the brief worry she'd had in Margie Wilson's café about not wanting her baby to see him with anyone other than her, she hadn't thought about Ash being available to other women, just free to devote himself to the foundation. And she was coming to realize that the idea didn't sit well.

Actually, it rankled something fierce.

There was some consolation, though, in the fact that Ash seemed to have eyes only for her.

He was sitting with his back against the tree roots that rose up from the earth, his legs stretched out, but he sat up and crossed them in front of him so he could lean nearer to her. "It's not an introduction to someone else that I want," he answered, his tone dripping with insinuation that secretly delighted her.

Danny spared her having to respond to it, though, returning from his meal with Kansas's nieces and nephews to sneak up behind Ash and yank the ponytail he'd previously defended.

"Who's that back there?" Ash pretended to be surprised and outraged, grabbing the giggling little boy to roll him over his head and into his lap. "You know what I do to kids who pull my hair?" he demanded once he had him there. "I tickle them."

And that was just what he did.

Beth watched as the big man tormented her nephew only enough to elicit squirms and shrieks of delight. She appreciated how much attention he'd given the little boy all day, and it occurred to her that she'd never really seen how he behaved around kids for any length of time.

But he'd been good with Danny. Patient, kind; just firm enough to let the three-year-old know his limits, and as relaxed as someone who was not only experienced, but who genuinely liked children.

He'd be a good father, she realized with a new certainty, and it gave her heart such a tug to think that she might not be around to watch him play like that with their own son or daughter. That some other woman he was now available to might be the one to witness it. And never in her life had she wanted so badly to stamp her own brand on him.

"Maybe all that tickling isn't such a good idea right after he's eaten," she suggested, and even though it was true, it was also an attempt to ease her own discomfort. She'd *divorced* the man, for crying out loud. How could she suddenly be feeling so possessive?

She couldn't. She no longer had the right.

Ash stopped, held Danny upside down for a split second and then let him do a somersault onto the blanket.

"More," the little boy hollered, jumping into Ash's arms for a second round. But this time Ash diverted his energies into shooting trash into the sack, like balls into a basket.

By the time they had the whole supper mess cleaned up, Danny had something else on his mind. He frowned very seriously at Beth.

"Is there a baby in yer tummy like my cousin Billy says?" he asked dubiously.

"Yes, there is."

"An' can it talk and tell you secrets?"

Both Ash and Beth laughed.

"I don't think so," she answered.

"Yep, it can," he insisted, as if he knew something she didn't. "Billy says."

"You know," Ash added devilishly, "he could be right. I think I read something about that not long ago. Maybe we should have a listen," he suggested to the child, all the while grinning at Beth.

"Can we?" Danny asked, his green eyes wide with wonder.

"Sure we can, can't we?" Ash challenged her.

Beth ignored him and instead spoke directly to her nephew. "You couldn't hear anything, sweetheart. Babies can't talk until a long time after they're born."

"Let's see," he insisted, encouraged by Ash, who was clearly enjoying putting her on the spot.

Beth made a face at her former husband and then leaned back on her hands far enough to make her mounded middle available. "Okay, go ahead," she told Danny.

The three-year-old knelt down and put his ear to her stomach, listening intently. "I hear'd it!" he said after a minute.

Again Ash and Beth laughed.

"What did he say?" Ash asked, as if he honestly believed it.

"I dunno, but it was sum'thin'."

"Let's see if I can tell," Ash suggested, stretching out on his side and leaning his weight on one elbow.

"You can't do that," Beth said under her breath.

"We have to know what he's trying to tell us," he protested as Danny made way for him.

"Ash—"

"Shh..."

Beth glanced around nervously to see if anyone was looking but her concern was quickly replaced by a jolt of sensation as Ash's head pressed to her stomach. He cupped his hand around it, as if to hear better, but he was really giving her a subtle massage that only the two of them knew about.

Warm honey sluiced through her and made her forget that they were out in public. She couldn't resist watching him, drinking in the sight of his chiseled profile as she fought the urge to caress his head the way he caressed her belly.

Then, as if to say hello to its father, the baby gave a solid kick.

"Hear it?" Danny demanded at about the same time.

"I do," Ash assured him.

"Wa's it said?"

"Something about letting him out of there so he can see the fireworks."

"Well, let 'im out, Aunt Beth," Danny chastised.

"Sorry. I can't do that. The baby has to stay awhile longer, I'm afraid. Next year it can see the fireworks." Then she wiggled a little to let Ash know his time was up. "Now it's saying it needs to go to sleep," she added pointedly, because the longer Ash stayed like that, slowly, sensuously rubbing her, the more things he was awakening inside of her, things that she should absolutely not be feeling at that time and in that place.

He finally sat up, but his hand remained, still working its wonders.

"We better has ice cream now," Danny said very solemnly, and as if there had been some segue into it.

Beth was grateful for the suggestion of anything that would save her from herself and from Ash's arousing touch. "Ice cream?" she asked.

"I promised," Ash explained, finally dragging his hand away, though clearly with reluctance.

Or was it something else that caused him to slide his hand so lazily across the whole mound of her middle before actually letting her go? Maybe he was *trying* to turn her on.

Ash stood then and turned to help her to her feet. But what she needed more than ice cream was time to gather her wits. "I think I'll just wait here for you guys. Don't be long—the fireworks should start soon."

After finding out if she wanted something, Ash lifted Danny to his shoulders the same way Jackson had earlier in the day and headed across the park to the booth where ice cream was being sold.

Beth's gaze followed Ash the whole way.

And as she watched him, a shiver danced up her spine at just the thought of how right it had felt to have him touch her.

At how much more she craved.

And at just the idea that there could ever be someone else taking her place...

* * *

The fireworks were spectacular. By the time they began, Ash and Danny had had their ice cream, and Jackson had rejoined them all. To make room on the blanket—or so he claimed—Ash pulled Beth very close beside him, casually keeping his arm stretched along the tree's unearthed root behind her and urging her to lie back with him to more comfortably see the display.

She probably shouldn't have, but she did. And as beautiful as the lights bursting in the air were, the longer it went on, the more her senses tuned in to Ash lying next to her instead of what she was supposed to be paying attention to.

The lean, hard length of him was pressed ever so slightly to her side. His arm pillowed her head. His hand did a slow massage of her shoulder and reminded her of the more subtle one he'd given her stomach earlier. His deep, rich voice washed over her every time he praised a particularly impressive explosion. His after-shave lingered faintly to drift to her like the scents of a far-off forest.

What she wanted, she realized with the rapid rise in her heartbeat and the feeling that all her nerve endings had risen to the surface of her skin to tingle to life, was for them to be the only two people there at the moment. She wanted to turn to him, wrap her arms around his neck, meld herself to that exquisitely masculine body of his and make love with him for hours and hours....

"That's it," Jackson said just then, interrupting her fantasy.

Beth hadn't even seen the end of the fireworks; she hadn't realized she'd been lost in her own thoughts and imaginings for so long. But the sky was quiet and smoky, and all around them blankets and picnic gear were being gathered, letting her know it really was over.

Then she heard Ash say to her brother, "Go ahead and get that boy home to bed. Beth and I can collect all this stuff and I'll drive her back."

Forcing herself to sit up, away from Ash and his effect on her, she glanced at Jackson, who was holding a very sleepy Danny on his lap.

"You don't have to do that," her brother answered Ash's offer. "It'll only take a minute to clean up, and then you won't have to come all the way out to the ranch."

But Ash wouldn't have it any other way, and even though Beth knew it was dangerous to accept his offer when she was all churned up inside, she finally ended the debate by siding with him.

Jackson accepted her decision without any more protest, said good-night and carried Danny off. But he'd been right about it not taking any time at all to gather their things, shake out the blanket and join the weary exodus from the park, because he was barely out of sight by the time they had finished.

"We could have packed up in the time we argued about who I was going home with and saved you the trip," Beth mused as they walked to the lodge to get Ash's car.

"What makes you think I wanted to be saved the trip?" Ash asked in a husky voice for her ears only.

Not much more was said after that. Unlike the previous evening, they didn't have the street to themselves, but even if they had, Beth would have been a little uneasy about pursuing an explanation of his intentions and discovering his train of thought was on the same treacherous track as hers.

As they reached the lodge, the crowd around them thinned. Beth wondered if Ash would again invite her into his cabin.

And if he did, if she'd go.

Because if she went, she knew that this time it wouldn't be for just a half hour of conversation.

But her wondering was all for naught, because Ash went straight to his car, pulling his keys from his pocket this time instead of needing to go inside to get them.

"Are you tired?" he asked when he'd put the picnic things into the back seat and they were both in the car.

Tired? No, she wasn't tired. Her wandering imagination during the fireworks had left her wide-awake. "It's not really late," she answered a little vaguely.

He tossed her a rakish smile and a sidelong glance that seemed to say more than words. "Are you in a hurry to get home?"

Something purely sensual skittered up her spine. "No," she said in a voice three octaves higher than normal. She cleared her throat. "Did you have something in mind?"

"As a matter of fact, I do."

He didn't offer any more information, and once again she was afraid to ask for fear of appearing too eager. What if she was misreading his intentions based on her own thoughts and feelings during the fireworks? After all, his room would have been a better choice if he was thinking and feeling what she was.

Neither of them spoke as he drove out of town, and when he reached the road that led up to the ranch house, he went past it, going about half a mile farther out before he turned onto a dirt path that would take them to a small, secluded lake on Heller property.

"I'm surprised you remember this," Beth said when she realized where he was headed. "I brought you here only once, the first time you came to meet Shag."

"It's one of my better memories of your old hometown."

That surprised her. She'd have guessed just the opposite.

The lake was a mile across and two wide, surrounded by a soft, loamy beach and pine trees that grew all the way to the water in some spots. Their relationship had been new that single other time they were there. And Beth had been embarrassed by what had happened just before they'd come. She didn't remember anything else about it, and she certainly couldn't think why it would be memorable for him.

Ash stopped the car at the end of the road and turned off the engine. He removed his shoes and socks, leaving them on the floorboard, then grabbed the picnic blanket from the back seat and got out.

Beth expected him to do or say something that included her. But he didn't come around to her side or so much as invite her to go with him, and she had the sense that she was being given a silent choice.

To leave the car and join him was to accept that tonight there would be no stopping short when passion flared between them, as surely it would. If she didn't want it to happen, she knew she'd better not get out.

She watched Ash in the distance, spreading the blanket near the water's edge. He sat in the center of it, his legs stretched in front of him, his upper body braced back on his hands. Then he tilted his face up to the star-filled sky as if greeting the moon.

And the moon answered by christening him in a silvery glow, reflecting off the sharp crests of his bones and leaving deep shadows in the hollows. He looked regally primitive, elemental, so in sync with nature's beauty and grace that it was difficult to picture him ever sitting behind a desk or dressed in an expensive English suit.

And what he was waiting for, she knew, was for her to shed all of her own self-imposed restraints to let nature take the course it had been so strongly striving for since he'd shown up here.

But could she do that?

Letting go to enjoy his company in the middle of a whole town full of people was one thing. But this was very different. To do this she would have to ignore what was in their past. To forbid herself to think of the dark tunnel of their future. To allow him to see that she really did still care for him . . .

If she stayed in the car, she felt sure he'd just come back. That he wouldn't say anything. That he wouldn't act as if she'd rejected him.

But they'd both know she had. That she'd closed a door he'd opened for them again.

That he really wasn't hers anymore . . .

A single click and the car door opened.

She kicked off her shoes and left them on the floor, just the way Ash had his, swinging her bare feet to the ground and getting out. She closed the door behind her carefully, as if not to disturb the night, and went to join him on the blanket.

Sitting down with her legs curled to the side, she studied his profile. He went on looking at the sky in stone-statue stillness, as if he were hardly aware of her. Though she knew that couldn't be true, because why else would he be smiling that small, pleased smile?

"How can this place have a good memory for you when we came out here after Shag had blasted our getting married?" she asked, as if no time at all had lapsed in their conversation.

His handsome face turned to her then, that smile stretching a bit wider. "It was the only time you ever said you loved me. Not directly, of course, you never did that. But in the process of railing about your father and his poorly concealed prejudice, you said that no matter what he thought, you loved me and were going to marry me."

"I said it other times," she claimed, though without much conviction, because she knew she hadn't been very forthcoming with those sentiments. It just wasn't her way.

"No," he corrected evenly, "you said 'me, too' when I said it. Or 'same here.' Or 'thanks'—that was the worst," he added, but with enough levity to take the sting out of it. "But you never looked me in the eye and said 'I love you.'"

And apparently that had had an impact on him, on their whole marriage, since he'd believed the reason she wanted the divorce was because she not only didn't say it, but didn't feel it, either.

"I'm sorry," she said, unsure how else to respond. But she could sense that it was inadequate. "I did, though," she added in a barely audible voice, staring out at the lake over her shoulder because she was too uncomfortable to venture it while she was looking at him. "Is that why you'd been thinking about divorce yourself—because you thought I didn't love you?"

"That, and because I was so damn frustrated with the fact that you never let me in—emotionally. When your father died and you wouldn't come out of that bathroom, when you wouldn't let me comfort you . . . I guess I just started to wonder what the hell we were doing together at all."

His words hung there between them as Beth let them sink in, as surprised by this as he'd been by her reasons for wanting to end the marriage. Not only was it nearly impossible for her to let anyone see her weaknesses, but she'd believed she was doing him a service by sparing him the sight.

Then Ash interrupted her thoughts. "So, if you honestly did love me then, what about now?"

"Now everything is confused," she said without having to think about it, because she was so lost in just that.

She could feel him watching her, waiting. She knew he wanted her to say more. That he wanted her to say she loved him, that she always had.

But she couldn't, especially not now when they weren't even married, when everything between them was so ambiguous, so uncertain.

After a moment, he seemed to let her off the hook. "I know for a fact that I want you," he said with a note of hopefulness in his voice, as if maybe he could get her to admit that much.

But still the best she could do was, "I guess that's what we're doing out here, isn't it?"

"I guess it is."

Then stop all this talking, and—

He raised a palm to her cheek and brought her face back to him. He searched her eyes with his, captured them, held them, conveyed with the solemnity of that gaze that he meant business here, that she'd better be willing to go the distance this time.

But she didn't need to think about it any more than she already had. She'd made that decision before she got out of the car. So she merely reached up and covered his hand with hers.

He waited another moment, as if wondering if she'd pull his hand away. But when she didn't, he brought her toward him and pressed his mouth to hers in the sweet nectar of the kiss she was craving.

His lips parted over hers, urging hers open, too, so his tongue could unite them, and before she knew it, she was lying on the soft, blanket-covered earth with Ash beside her, his big body partly over her, lost in the hungry, yearning play that told her she hadn't been the only one having fantasies this evening.

He crossed a heavy thigh over her lap and Beth let her hand rest on it, reveling in the feel of the power there as wanton images flitted through her mind.

Somewhere deep down, she'd known this night would end like this. Or at least hoped it would.

Her back arched toward Ash's chest, and she let go of his thigh to wrap her arms around him, to pull herself up to him and feel the pressure of her breasts against that solid expanse.

But that was apparently not what he had in mind, for his hand left its caress of her face to slide down her neck to her shoulder, and on to her breast, outside of her clothes.

Much better, she had to admit as he began to work his magic there. Better still when he finally slipped inside to cup her bare skin and let her nipple grow taut in his palm. In fact, it felt so good, it took her breath away. She tore from their kiss and let her head drop back, inviting him to occupy his mouth in other pursuits.

He kissed his way down the column of her throat as he made quick work of the buttons of her dress, exposing her heated flesh to the night air and then to his seeking, moist mouth.

And even though she'd known that was where he was headed, the sensation was almost too glorious to bear.

Teasing, tormenting, sucking, circling her nipple with his tongue, even gently nipping and tugging with his teeth. Every stroke tightened a cord of pleasure inside her, a cord he strummed at just the right moments, with just the right touch.

She needed him to be closer, so much closer....

Suddenly their clothes seemed to be a barrier Ash couldn't abide one moment more, either. He abandoned her to tear off his shirt, to fling his jeans away, and then to undress her in the same flurry of impatience. When he came back to her, it was to press his warm, taut, naked body to hers with a new urgency....

Urgency in his mouth on hers again, briefly, before it reclaimed her breast. Urgency in his hand exploring her belly for only a moment before he reached below and found the core of her yearning for him. Urgency in his long, hard shaft finding that same spot to slip inside her in what, by then, they were both straining for—that one perfect union, which would join them so completely that nothing that had ever separated them would matter.

Slowly, carefully, his thrusts spoke of his concern for her, for her condition, until Beth met and matched him and showed him how much more she wanted. How much more she needed.

His hands were in her hair, his mouth savored hers, until passion ignited into flames too consuming for anything but riding the storm.

And when it crested, her climax was so incredible she cried out as she never had, clinging to the solid wall of muscle that was Ash's back, wrapping her legs around him to hold him buried deeply inside of her as wave after wave of the most intense pleasure lifted her higher and higher until she thought she might burst.

Then, just as the waves began to settle her back to earth, Ash's whole body tensed above her, inside her, plunging in deeper still, forcefully, giving her not only more of the seed that had already sprouted in her womb but a second tremor of ecstasy to ripple through her until each thrust grew slower, calmer, and finally exhausted itself and them along with it.

Ash settled atop her. Keeping some of his weight on his arms braced on either side of her head, he looked down into her eyes again, holding them as surely as he held her.

And somewhere far out on the periphery of the pleasure he'd given her, the contentment she felt, she waited for him to complete it all by saying he loved her, the way he usually did at that moment. Not only because she craved hearing the words, but because if only he'd say it, she thought *she* might be able to, too.

But he didn't.

And without it, she couldn't.

Instead he slid his arms beneath her as his body slipped out of hers and he rolled to his back, holding her close to his side.

"Are you all right?" he asked, his breath a hot gust in her hair. "I didn't mean to be so rough, but—"

"I'm fine. You're never too rough," she assured him quietly.

He cupped the back of her head and held it to his heart, cherishing her even without the words, and she felt each of his muscles relax in turn, the way they did when he was falling asleep.

But somehow, even as wonderful as their lovemaking had been, it seemed incomplete. It was the words that were missing, she knew.

She waited, but those words never came. And then she heard his breathing deepen and knew that hole would not be filled. Not by him. Because he really had gone to sleep.

The stars glittered in the sky above them. The water moved just beyond them in a soft ripple. The moon bathed them. The soft earth cradled them. And she had the odd sense that all of nature was waiting, even if he wasn't.

"I love you, Ash," she whispered so softly even she barely heard it.

And as she finally drifted toward sleep, she wondered if he'd always felt what she did at that moment laying bare her feelings and getting nothing in return.

Because it was a loneliness as painful as any she'd ever known.

Chapter Nine

Sometime during the night Beth had rolled to her other side and Ash had apparently followed, because she woke to the feel of warm, early morning sunshine and him curved perfectly behind her.

That wasn't what lured her from sleep, though. What did that was his hand, moving in a slow caress of her stomach. And the sense that she was being watched. Or studied, actually, from where he'd propped his head up on his hand to peer over at her.

And while the changes in her body were not enormous or unsightly, and had some positive aspects, she wasn't comfortable having them all so openly assessed in broad daylight.

She reached for the edge of the blanket and pulled it around her as she turned to glance at him. "Looks like we camped out."

"Looks like it," he agreed, his smile mischievous, as if he knew how uneasy she felt and was enjoying her modesty. He didn't do anything to stop her from covering herself, but he also didn't stop his sensual exploration of her middle underneath the blanket. "I was enjoying myself, you know."

"When?"

"Just now. Looking at you. There are some interesting things happening to you."

She glanced further over her shoulder and downward at him, and even though she couldn't really see anything, she said, "You look the same," with enough impudence to hide her own discomfort.

"Is that bad?"

"No," she admitted, unable to suppress an appreciative grin at just the thought.

Before she realized what he was doing, Ash flung the blanket away and pressed her to her back. "Your changes aren't bad, either. In fact, I'd say they're pretty terrific."

She tried to retrieve the blanket again, but one long arm shot out across her, caught her wrist and held it captive while he sat up some, still braced on his elbow but with his head raised, the better to see her. He began a slow scrutiny that seemed to memorize every new curve.

"They're all very sexy," he said in a quiet, husky voice that relayed his admiration. "And this . . ." he went on, his gaze dropping to the evidence of his baby. "This is what we made together. I could look at it forever," he said, finishing in awe, just before he bent over and placed a kiss above her navel.

Then he let go of her wrist and, in one lithe movement, sat up, swung a leg over her to straddle her, and cupped her stomach with one big hand on either side of it. "Incredible," he whispered, exploring, kneading, learning every inch of that small, firm mound with his hands and eyes as if to convince himself it was real, that what was growing inside of it was real.

Embarrassment warred in Beth with the rekindling of desires she thought had been well sated just hours before. She reached his thighs with both hands, considering whether to push him away. But once she felt those solid, muscular legs, the decision made itself and she did some caressing of her own instead.

"We should get dressed before somebody happens out here," she said, but it was a feeble suggestion that Ash didn't even seem to hear.

Instead his eyes had returned to her breasts, and a devilish smile played on his lips as he raised his hands from her middle and filled them with her new voluptuousness. "Oh, yeah, this is *very* nice. And would you look at that—all I have to do is say hello and they perk right up for me."

"You have no room to talk," she countered, finding the advantage to the situation in her own view of his body in broad daylight. He was gloriously, magnificently naked, wearing only the arrowhead tied around his neck and a clear indication much lower down that he wanted her. Again.

She slid her hands to midthigh but let her eyes go farther up his body to that long, thick shaft; to his flat belly; to the widening V of his torso; to his broad, powerful shoulders; to his exquisitely masculine face.

And, heaven help her, she wanted him, too. Again.

She paused for a moment. "In case you've forgotten, we're not far from the house, where at this moment, my brother and any number of ranch hands are getting ready to go to work. Depending on the direction they take, that could mean they'll pass right by here.''

"I guess we'll have to hurry then," he answered with a sly smile that said he wasn't worried.

But then, neither was she. Not really. Not when he cradled her face and kissed her, setting aflame the passions that were so eager to be reignited it was as if they hadn't been satisfied at all.

Neither Ash nor Beth moved with any haste. They made love slowly, as if they had all day there in the sun, relearning the sight of each other the way their hands had already relearned the feel.

Beth's inhibitions about her body melted away. How could she stay self-conscious when Ash found such delight in it and in turn raised her own levels of pleasure to new heights?

He kissed her everywhere, following the path of his hands to trail every inch of her skin, awakening her nerve endings and bringing them all to the surface to sizzle to life. And along with the smooth, unbroken line of his exploration there was a playfulness, a teasing, a delicious torment that had her writhing in response.

In the light of day and their rediscovered familiarity, Beth gave as good as she got. He was a physically incredible man, and while it was easy to forget that in the cloak of darkness, now she feasted on it.

Her hands slid along the taut, burnished flesh of his shoulders, so wide her arms could hardly span them. She rode the bulge of his biceps with her flattened palms and kissed her way from one hard pectoral to the other while her hands rounded his narrow waist and slipped down to that derriere that caught her eye whenever his back was turned.

He was ticklish and she knew just the spot on his side to tease with her tongue to make him squirm, not minding at all when he got even with the flick of his own tongue in secret places that drove her wild.

And this time when passion grew too great to bear, she reached for him with both hands, reveling in the feel of that thick, hard shaft for a moment before guiding it home to fill the gaping emptiness as only he could.

She surrendered to the intensity of his thrusts then, letting him take her higher and higher, climbing until they reached their peak together, their breaths mingling, their bodies melded into one in an ecstasy so intense Beth could only cling to him, welcoming the full length of him so deeply inside of her that more than their bodies were joined—their spirits and hearts seemed to be, too.

But as much as she wanted it to go on forever, nothing that powerful could last, and finally they both crossed over the crest, slowly, slowly floating back to earth. To reality.

"I love you," Ash said into her hair in a ragged voice.

Beth smiled, truly feeling replete now, as she hadn't the night before. "I love you, too," she whispered back.

Ash pushed up on his hands and stared down at her. "What did you say?"

He wasn't going to make this easy for her. And it *wasn't* easy for her. Especially not if she had to look at him and repeat it or discuss it. Why couldn't he just let it lie?

"Beth?" he coaxed.

But she didn't know if she could say it again. If she could let him scrutinize her emotions the same way he'd studied her body.

She swallowed with some difficulty and tried. "I said I love you, too," she managed, though so softly it was a hushed whisper this time.

His supple mouth stretched into a leisurely smile that stretched into a full-fledged grin. "I'll be damned. I didn't think I'd ever hear that from you."

Then they were even—sort of—because she'd been afraid she might not ever hear it from him again, either.

He laughed wryly. "It's all the wrong way around, you know," he said, slipping from her and rolling to his side to prop his head on his hand once more.

"What is?"

"Everything about us. We got married before we really knew each other, and only after we divorced are we having a baby and are you finally telling me you love me. We should have met, gotten to know each other, *shared our feelings*, married, *shared our feelings*, and had a baby. And maybe skipped the divorce altogether."

His repetition of the sharing their feelings part nettled her as nothing in the soft earth under the blanket had. But she didn't want to fight, so she ignored it. "We certainly seem to have jumbled everything up," she agreed.

"Maybe it's time we straighten them out," he suggested in a quiet voice of his own, as if venturing into dangerous territory.

"Have you mastered the art of time travel to send us back to do it over?" she joked, for some reason feeling terribly vulnerable and pulling her side of the blanket over her again.

"I'm talking about making it right from here on," Ash said.

An odd mixture of feelings bubbled inside her at that moment. She had a pretty good idea what he was leading up to, and a part of her hoped she was right.

But another part of her hoped she wasn't.

With the blanket held tightly in place across her breasts, she sat up and looked at him, lying there in all his glory, staring past her out at the lake, as if he were gauging whether he really wanted to say what he was about to.

Then he turned his sharp-boned face up to her. "Maybe we should take a second stab at marriage."

Was he unsure of the wisdom in it? Or how she might react to the suggestion? Or was it that he didn't really want to? Because there was clearly uncertainty in his tone.

And that uncertainty fed the portion of her that had hoped a proposal was *not* what he'd been leading up to.

But she cared for this man and she was having his baby. And those two things kept her from doing or saying anything rash.

What they couldn't keep her from was voicing her own doubts. "I'm not sure that's a good idea."

He chuckled a little and sat up, raising one leg to brace an elbow on. "Well, at least that isn't a no. Let's talk about it."

Beth couldn't feel easy about either the idea of remarriage or the discussion of it. "I think we ought to get dressed first."

"You're stalling," he said, doubts creeping into his voice. "Surely this is something you must have thought about."

Not in a way that actually considered it. But she didn't say that.

And before she could say anything at all, he went on "What worries you most about the idea of our getting married again?"

"What worries *you* most?" she countered. "You didn't exactly propose with gusto. And if the only rea son you did was because you feel some sort of obligation—"

"I'll meet my *obligations* to the baby whether we're married or not," he cut her off. "I'm not talking about some shotgun wedding here. I'm talking about our getting back together because we both want to."

"All right then, what worries you most?" she repeated.

His frown was dark enough to let her know he was indeed worried, about more than whether or not she might reject his proposal. When he finally answered, it was as if he were choosing his words very carefully. "I can't say I'm comfortable with the fact that we'd be going back into something we already failed at."

She understood that well, because she had the same trepidation. But she could tell by the deepening of the lines between his bushy brows that there was more to it than his generalization. And that the details carried the most weight. "Go on," she urged and challenged at once.

He shook his head dubiously. "I, uh, don't know if you'll ever really be able to open up to me, to let me know what I need to know—good and bad—before just up and bailing out altogether."

He was being honest, and she knew she should be grateful for that. But what she wanted—deep down in that woman's heart her father had taught her to hide away—was for him to sweep her off her feet the way he had when they'd met. To tell her he loved her too much to live without her, no matter what had gone wrong before. To swear there wasn't a doubt in his mind that they could make it this time. That nothing would come between them. And she wanted him to do it all with so much conviction that even she would be convinced.

What she didn't want was a complaint that felt as if he were blaming her for the failure of their marriage.

But that's what she was getting.

Then, as if he read her mind, he reached over and took her free hand, rubbing the back of it in small circles with his thumb in a gesture that was soothing and sexy and sweetly romantic at the same time. "But we do love each other," he went on. "And it wasn't as if our marriage was horrible. There were a lot of good things about it. Good things between us. Good times."

That was all true. She couldn't dispute it.

"And there's the baby now, too," he added. "I'm not feeling I have some duty to marry you because you're pregnant, but the baby's a factor here. I want us to raise this child together. I don't want to be alone in the joy of it and feeling bad that you aren't there to see or experience something terrific. And I sure as hell don't want to be wondering what's happening that I'm not a part of. We've created a family, Beth, and I think that's what we should be. It's what I want us to be."

She agreed with that, too. But still, that woman's heart was tweaked. "If there wasn't going to be a baby, though, you wouldn't be here right now. You wouldn't even be thinking about our remarrying."

"Don't be too sure. I wasn't happy about the divorce."

"Oh, really? You seemed more than willing to me."

"It was you who said you wanted it."

"And you who said you'd been thinking the same thing. And then moved out of the house so fast you made my head spin."

He was still holding her hand, but he wasn't rubbing it anymore. "I thought that was what you wanted. Was divorce just a ploy? Are you telling me I called your bluff?''

"No, of course not." But it might have hurt less if he'd hesitated even a little. If he hadn't seemed so eager to be rid of her...

"Just don't pretend that you didn't want the divorce, too, when you made it very clear that you did."

He took a deep breath and sighed it out. "I couldn't have made it very clear that I wanted the divorce, because I *wasn't* very clear that I did. I said I'd been *thinking* about it myself."

"And then you hurried to move out," she repeated.

"You wouldn't talk to me about it!" he nearly shouted, his frustration sounding. "And if you'll recall, I also suggested marriage counseling before we actually filed for divorce, but you refused that, too. You said talking wouldn't do anything and you weren't letting some perfect stranger poke around in your psyche. What choice did that leave? You wanted out and that was that. But it doesn't mean I was happy about it. And I've been even less happy about the reality of it."

"Meaning?"

"Meaning that I've missed you, damn it! I've missed coming home late at night and finding you all soft and warm in bed. I've missed Sunday mornings—making love, having breakfast together, reading the newspaper. I've missed being able to call you when I start craving the sound of your voice. And knowing you'll be there waiting for me when I get back from someplace. And knowing you're my wife and picturing us growing old together. I've missed... hell, I've missed just about everything."

Just about everything. But not everything.

Well, she'd missed a lot of things, too. But missing Ash wasn't anything new to her. All those same evenings he was so happy to come home and find her soft and warm in bed were the evenings she'd spent alone and lonely before she'd fallen asleep.

And how many Sunday mornings wasn't he there to make love to her and have breakfast with her and read the newspapers, when he was either out of town or already up and gone to the office or taking care of something else that needed him? She'd missed him then, too. Just the way she had through all of that time he'd been so happy to know she was waiting for him.

And even being married to him hadn't allowed her to simply call to hear the sound of his voice when she craved it, because at the other end of the line would be either no answer or an intimidating Miss Lightfeather telling her he was unavailable.

Unavailable.

He'd missed her not being available to him since the divorce, but he hadn't been available to her in a long, long time.

"And I've missed playing Boat," he interrupted her thoughts, smiling at the memory and apparently overlooking the fact that she was not feeling lighthearted at the moment. "Not to mention making love to you the way I did last night and just now."

She smiled, too, but just for a moment. Finally she blurted out what was on her mind. "Would it be any different?" And her woman's heart listened very carefully, hoping that having let him know two days before why she'd divorced him had given him the clue to what to say, to what she wanted—needed—from him, and that he'd tell her everything would be better, that he'd make her and the baby his first priority...

"What do you mean?" he asked.

"A second marriage. What would change to make it work now when it didn't before?" she prompted.

"That's what we'd have to hash out, beginning with your being up-front with me about what's going on inside that head of yours."

Beth's heart took cover even as she prompted again. "Okay, let's say I start blathering about every little thought or feeling I have. What then?"

He frowned. "Then we work on what's wrong."

"I already told you what was wrong. You were gone all the time. I was just a pit stop in your life. How will you fix that?"

"I can't give you a blanket answer for what I'll do. It'll have to be something I deal with as each thing comes up."

"And how would that be any different from before? Except maybe that as you're leaving, you'll know I'd rather you weren't?"

"What are you saying? That you'd want me to turn my back on the foundation? On my other responsibilities? On my work?"

Beth just stared at him, wondering why it was so important for her to lay bare all her feelings when doing it didn't accomplish anything.

"No, I'm not saying I want you to turn your back on the foundation. I know what you do is important," she finally answered him. "But don't you see, Ash? The demands on you will be the same. And I think your response to them will be, too—you'll meet them all. And that will leave the baby and me at the bottom of the list."

He looked as if she were asking the impossible of him. "Maybe I could set aside some specific time for us—like a standing appointment, if that's what you mean," he finally said. "Or I could bring some work home so I can be available to you if you need me. Or try keeping the traveling to a minimum . . ."

But there was so much hedging in what he said, he didn't sound confident enough to convince himself, let alone her.

He'd have good intentions, Beth thought. He'd make a stab at putting their marriage before the foundation work, but demands would press in on him. Crises would happen. And he'd be off again.

"Remember," he put in, "you'll have the baby, too. You'll be busier than you were before. Part of the time you won't even notice I'm gone."

There was something about that that rubbed her the wrong way. Something that she thought made her sound so needy and weak and dependent that he had to be pointing out what could occupy and entertain her.

She let out a mirthless little laugh. "So let me see if I have this straight. You believe that the real problem in our marriage was that I didn't announce what I was thinking and feeling every minute—"

"It isn't as if I'm blaming that for everything," he amended with no small amount of heat in his voice. "But I'll repeat what I said the other day—I can't fix what I don't know is broken. When you don't tell me what bothers you, how the hell am I supposed to know you're bothered?"

"But I *let* you know what bothered me. And the best you can do with it is say you'll try to be around a little more, but you're warning me even as you say it that nothing is likely to change, except that the baby will fill my time like a hobby."

"I don't know what else I can say except that I'll try to spend more time with you," he said impatiently, angrily.

Beth cringed. He sounded as if he were answering an old harridan's nagging. And she didn't like being cast as the nagging old harridan.

With her dignity stiffening her spine, Beth let go of the blanket and found her clothes to put on as if they were armor to bolster and protect her. "I just don't think so," she said then.

"You don't think what?"

"That our getting married again would work. It wouldn't be any different than it was before, except that there'd be the baby. What was wrong would still be wrong."

"And we'd have to work to make it right," he said in measured tones that announced he didn't like her answer.

"All the work in the world won't change the fact that you're constantly needed elsewhere. That there will always be something bigger and more important to take care of, something that can be dealt with only by you. And you'll be gone. And I'll be there. Waiting. Putting things off—putting off my whole life—until you have time for me."

"Damn it, Beth—"

"You know it's true. You've just said it yourself, in so many words."

"I said I'd try—"

"But trying won't change the fact that you need to do the work of three people. That you just plain don't have room in your life for marriage." Her voice cracked and it took her a moment to fix it before she could finish. And even then the sadness tinged it. "I won't marry you again, Ash."

"You're ignoring the good things. What about last night and this morning?" he demanded angrily. "What about the baby? The fact that we care about each other?"

"It isn't enough," she answered in a near whisper, because she wished it was.

Then she went to the car, put on her shoes, and began walking in the direction of the house.

"Where the hell are you going?" he shouted to her.

"Home," she called, salvaging what was left of her pride by not looking at him. She couldn't bear even the thought that he might see all the emotions that were tearing her apart.

"Damn it, Beth!" he said again. "Come back here and talk to me about this!"

But she just kept going, telling herself that no matter how much she didn't want it to be true, there was no future for them together.

And she could only assume that in spite of Ash's protestations, he knew it, too.

Because he didn't follow.

Chapter Ten

What the hell did she want from him? Ash railed silently as he drove to the lodge in the glare of morning's first sunshine after watching Beth walk away from the lakeside where they'd spent the night. And made love. And argued...

She said that she didn't want to interfere with his work, that she knew it was important. But then she crucified him for it.

She didn't expect him to turn his back on the foundation. But anything short of that and she wouldn't marry him again.

What more could he do than promise to try to cut back some?

And what had she offered to change?

Had she said she'd try being more open about her feelings so he could know what was going on with her? So he could be warned when she felt as if he hadn't been around enough? So he could be alerted that he'd done something wrong?

No, she hadn't, not in anything more than a hypothetical scenario.

And what about the positive things she might be feeling? Had she said she'd work at letting him in on those, either?

No, she hadn't.

This was just like her—walking away from a problem rather than hammering at it until it was solved. Was that what she thought he should do with everything the foundation had to deal with—give nothing more than a lame attempt to fix it and then forget it? If it was too tough, too complicated, too messy, just bury it and leave?

Because he couldn't do that.

And he wished to God she couldn't, either, so that maybe they'd still be at that lake, figuring out a way to deal with their problems, to get back together, to be a family.

But no. She'd left. Basically, the same way she'd bailed out of their marriage.

He barreled into the lodge parking lot so fast the turn was nearly on two wheels and his tires squealed when he came to a stop in front of his cabin.

For a moment he considered backing out again and heading for the ranch. But it wouldn't do any more good to go after her now than it would have when she'd first taken off, and he knew it. Not when she was on her high horse like that, all closed off and impervious. She was never easy to reach, but when she put up that wall to hide her feelings behind, it was useless to even think about breaching it.

Besides, he was too frustrated and irritated to be rational or reasonable himself. He'd only make things worse.

So rather than retracing his tracks, he jammed the car into park and turned off the engine.

But he still didn't rush to get out. Instead, he sat there, staring at the small rustic cabin and wondering what the hell he was going to do.

He loved her.

He wanted her.

He wanted the baby.

He wanted them both in his life full-time.

But the foundation and all it entailed was a part of that life.

"Damn it!" he shouted, hitting the steering wheel with both hands.

He was disgusted. With himself. With Beth. With everything.

He finally shoved the car door open, got out and slammed it shut again. Hard.

Not that it made him feel any better, but if he didn't vent some of his anger and frustration somehow, he was liable to drive out to that ranch the way he was itching to and vent it at Beth.

He stabbed his key into the lock on the cabin door and threw it wide. In the gust of air that went with it, several small sheets of paper rose up from the floor like leaves in the wind, scattering back down to the nubby gray carpet.

He bent over to gather them, realizing as he did that they were phone messages that had been slipped under the door.

They were all from his grandfather, and with a wave of alarm he read through them in a hurry.

The time each call had been received was noted. All but one of them had come in late the day before and into the evening. The last was marked just half an hour ago.

Each one relayed a little more information, a little more urgency.

Serious charges were being levered against the drug and alcohol rehabilitation center the foundation had built and overseen.

An impromptu investigation was under way by hostile officials.

There were threats to close the place. To have the director arrested.

His grandfather thought he'd better get back there on the double. . . .

"Perfect," Ash muttered to himself. "Absolutely perfect."

And he could have sworn the gods were laughing at him.

Beth had fallen on the walk from the lake to the house that morning.

Lost in thoughts of Ash and how stubborn he was, she missed spotting a gopher hole, stepped into it and gone down. Not hard. At least she hadn't thought so. Just enough to scrape a knee. Certainly not like some of the spills she'd taken as a kid, working the ranch.

She'd gotten to her feet, brushed herself off and walked the rest of the way, counting herself lucky that she hadn't broken or sprained anything.

It wasn't until that afternoon that the cramping started.

At first she hadn't even connected it with the fall. Then, when she remembered it, she thought maybe it had just caused some muscle spasms, because that's all it felt like. Nothing serious. And it would disappear. It was so mild she didn't pay it any mind.

Then, at four-thirty, she started to spot. Lightly, but unmistakably. And that was when she began to consider that the fall had been more jarring than she'd realized and she wasn't just having muscle spasms. She also finally admitted to herself that she wasn't just a kid coming in from chores with a scraped knee.

She was a pregnant woman who might be having labor pains.

Ash had been on her mind all day, but when it occurred to her that the baby could be in jeopardy she forgot about their fight. She just plain wanted him by her side.

After notifying the doctor's office of what was happening and telling them she was on her way in, she dialed Ash's cabin at the lodge. But there was no answer and when even her call to the front desk wasn't picked up, she was afraid of spending any more time trying to track him down.

Instead, she left a note letting Jackson know there was a problem with the baby, that she'd gone into town to the doctor, and asking him to please try reaching Ash to tell him.

Then she got in her car and headed for Elk Creek's medical facility without even considering that maybe she shouldn't drive.

That only dawned on her when it began to seem as if the pains were coming stronger and closer together.

Or did it just seem that way because now that she knew what they were she was alert to every twinge?

What if she lost the baby? she started to wonder.

Oh, Lord, she couldn't think about that. It made her heart beat even faster than it was, her hands shake more. Her whole body turn into an even tighter cord of stress.

What have I done? What have I done? she kept asking herself, wishing she'd never stormed off with no thought to anything but her pride and getting away from Ash before he could see how much she'd wanted him, how hurt and sad and disappointed she'd been.

Please don't let anything happen to the baby. Please. And please send Ash. Send him right away....

Because she was more afraid than she'd been in her whole life, and if ever she'd needed anyone at any time, it was Ash right then.

Ash didn't reach the reservation until late that afternoon. He went straight to his office, finding Miss Lightfeather closing up for the day.

She paused long enough to fill him in—a teenage patient at the rehab center had convinced his parents that atrocities were being committed by the director. The parents had pressured authorities to look into it and at that moment state investigators were at the rehab center in the second phase of their inquiry.

"My grandfather?" Ash asked in a kind of shorthand.

"He's at the center, too, though I don't know what he can do. It's *you* who needs to be there," the dour-faced woman pointed out.

"I'm on my way," he answered, turning toward the door he'd just come through.

"It's good that you're back," she called after him. "There's an awful stack of other things that have to have your attention, too. ASAP."

Ash waved a hand in the air to let her know he'd heard, but he didn't pause to respond.

The rehab center wasn't far from his office. He made it there in five minutes and was told where he needed to be by the volunteer at the admissions desk without even having to ask.

He found the team of four investigators in the basement with his grandfather and the center's very worried looking director. Both men's faces showed relief when they caught sight of Ash, and within moments he had taken over, doing what he did best—dealing with the problem.

And immersing himself in work without another thought to anything else.

"You're looking tired, old man," Ash said as he poured himself and his grandfather coffee in the doctor's lounge while the investigators went through the director's files and journals later that night.

"Humph. Tired of waiting," Robert answered, accepting the paper cup as Ash joined him at a round table.

His grandfather's long hair—like his—was tied in a leather strap at his nape, but unlike Ash's, it was a shock of pure white. And while they resembled each other, Robert Yazzie's face was lined and creased like a river bottom in a drought.

"It's past ten. Just because I persuaded these people to work late doesn't mean you have to stay. Why don't you go on home?" Ash suggested.

His grandfather ignored him. "Did you settle things with our little Beth?" he asked instead, clearly seizing the first chance he'd had since Ash had arrived to satisfy his curiosity.

Ash let out a mirthless half chuckle, half sigh. "I don't think you could call anything between us settled, no. I had a big fight with her this morning—I asked her to marry me again and she turned me down flat."

"Why?"

Ash explained, trying to keep the anger out of his voice. And failing.

"I'm surprised at Beth wanting you to give up the foundation," his grandfather said when he'd finished.

"She didn't say that in so many words. But I sure as hell can't see where she meant anything else. I said I'd cut back where I could, and she still wouldn't even consider our getting together again."

"Could be she doesn't believe you can do it."

Ash wasn't so quick to respond to that, because the tone in his grandfather's voice said the old man didn't believe it, either. "I know it'll be a hard promise to keep, but—"

"Or an impossible one. Over the years I've seen how much you've taken on for yourself through the foundation. Saw it even clearer being in your shoes since you went after her. You're a very busy man."

"There's always a lot of work. A lot of problems," Ash confirmed with a glance around them, silently citing their present situation as an example.

"And somebody has to see to it all," Robert put in.

"And that somebody is me," Ash finished. He'd been wondering all day and through the evening if this particular crisis was fate's way of telling him he was a fool to think he actually could reduce his work load or avoid being drawn away by emergencies in order to devote more time to his personal life.

"Guess you *could* close down the foundation," his grandfather said, as if he were ruminating on the idea.

"You know I can't do that." And Ash knew his grandfather wouldn't want him to.

Neither of them said anything for a moment. Then Robert broke the silence with a change of subject. "I've been wondering about you, you know."

"What have you been wondering about me?"

The old man shrugged. "Too many nights I played gin rummy with Beth while she watched the clock and looked out the window at every sound, hoping it was you. Too many times I watched her send you away with a smile, only to see that smile fade when you were gone. Too many times she trumped up excuses for me to visit just to keep away the loneliness. Too many times, Ash, and they all added up to the same thing—she didn't see enough of you. She missed you. But I never had the impression that you were missing her. Not until she ended the marriage. And I'm wondering why that is. If the little you saw her was all you really wanted of her."

Ash couldn't believe what his grandfather was implying. "You're wondering if I *liked* being away so much?"

Again the shrug, as if Robert thought it was possible. "*Did* you miss her when you were gone?"

Ash started to answer that, but then stopped, because an honest response wasn't as easy to come by as it should have been. "I was busy when I was gone and—" But again he stopped short at the sound of his own words. And the words he hadn't been able to say—that yes, he had missed her when he was away from her during their marriage.

Because for the most part, he hadn't.

Not then.

Staring into his coffee cup, he thought about what his grandfather was getting at.

He'd been missing Beth something fierce since they'd separated. But before that?

Before that he'd always known she'd be there whenever he managed to get home to her, and that had made him feel good. Great. After all, he'd had other things on his mind while he was away, and knowing where she was, what she was doing, that she was capable of caring for herself and he didn't need to worry about her...

Had made him take her for granted.

Wasn't that what it all amounted to?

He didn't want it to be true, but as if a light had been turned on in a dark room, he knew it was.

Now he suddenly wondered if the way he'd felt since he'd lost her was how she'd felt throughout their marriage.

Because if it was, it was no wonder she'd divorced him.

And it was also no wonder she'd been protective of herself and her feelings before that.

He'd put all the blame on her for being closed off emotionally. But if they'd just seen more of each other, if she hadn't been left feeling bad and hiding it behind assurances that she didn't mind his being gone so much, would she have eventually opened up to him in other ways?

He couldn't be sure, but it seemed possible.

It also occurred to him now that the simple fact of spending time together might have allowed him to feel closer to her whether she wore her heart on her sleeve or not. And that should have been something that came naturally with being married.

What had she said when she'd finally told him why she'd wanted a divorce? That it should have gone without saying that two people who were married to each other actually spent time together?

And she'd been right. She shouldn't have had to complain about rarely seeing him in order for him to recognize that it was a problem. To get him not to take her for granted. Not to neglect her. Because he *had* neglected her, he saw that now.

"I've been a first-class jerk, haven't I?" he finally said to his grandfather, who had sat silently through his soul-searching as if he could see the process.

Still the old man didn't say anything. He just stared at him the way he had when Ash was a boy, as if waiting for him to see the whole picture for himself.

"You knew, didn't you? You knew that I really had just made her a pit stop in my life the way she accused me. That all the while she was missing me and unhappy, I was too wrapped up in work to feel the same way. The divorce and what I've suffered since she said she wanted out was what I had coming, wasn't it? Because it was just what she suffered, and I was blind to it. I barely took it seriously when she came right out and told me about it a few days ago." Ash shook his head in self-disgust.

"Some lessons aren't easy to learn," Robert said.

"The trouble is," Ash added, feeling as fatalistic as he sounded "even if I got a second chance to appreciate her, the rest of the problem hasn't changed. There's still the foundation and all the demands on me."

"Guess you could close it down," his grandfather repeated.

"Why do you keep saying that?"

Robert shrugged once more, this time in a way that said *figure it out*. "Something has to give, Ash."

But before he could mull it over, they were interrupted by the center's director. The man poked his head through the lounge doorway and asked them to rejoin him and the investigators in his office.

"Think I'll go on home after all, and let you take it from here," Robert said as they stood to follow the director into the corridor.

But there was mischief in those old eyes and Ash saw it. He just couldn't explore it right then. "I'll call you when I get through here and let you know what happens," he said instead.

"Do that," Robert answered pointedly, heading for the front door.

Ash watched him as the old man made his way out of the building. There was nothing about the sight of that big, broad back, still straight and strong in spite of all the years it carried, to make him think his grandfather was up to something.

But Ash sensed that he was.

And that before too long, he'd find out about it.

The lights were on in his two-story adobe house when Ash got there after midnight. For one split second he had the unreasonable thought that it was Beth who was inside, the way she used to be.

But of course that was just wishful thinking.

The kitchen and side porch light of his grandfather's house next door were also on, and it was a pretty good bet Robert was who waited for him.

Ash put the car in the garage, grabbed his garment bag and briefcase from the back seat and went in through the door that opened into the laundry room.

There were no sounds coming from anywhere inside, but out in his backyard he could see a fire burning. Just a small one. At the end of a brick path that wound through the garden.

And there, standing nearby, was Robert, looking very pleased with himself. "Come on out," he called when he saw Ash.

None of the patio lights were on, but as Ash went into the yard, his grandfather moved to a pottery bowl on the ground not far from the main fire and lit another one inside it to flame to life, too.

"What are you doing, old man?" Ash asked.

Robert just smiled, moved to yet another spot and set a fairly large pile of kindling ablaze. Then he pointed to the pottery bowl. "Better put that out," he suggested. As Ash did, he said, "How'd things go at the center?"

"The investigators didn't give us a final verdict, but I think we're in the clear except for some overcrowding problems. Since they didn't find naked women chained to beds or torture chambers in the basement or records of sadistic experiments and tortures on inpatients, they were finally convinced that that boy was just stirring up trouble because he hadn't liked being sent to us. We're clean, and they saw that. Now I just have to come up with the funds for expansion or turn people away," he finished with a weary sigh for yet another major problem that he'd have to deal with.

"Ah, a new fire," Robert murmured, but Ash didn't know if he was referring to the one he'd just lit or to the need for more funds.

Robert brought to life three more small conflagrations, and now he pointed to two of them. "Better put those out."

Ash knew the old man well enough to know this was what had caused the glint in his eye earlier that evening. He just didn't know what the hell it was all about.

He smothered the other fires, but when he moved to snuff the main one at the end of the garden path, Robert stopped him. "Don't pay any attention to that one. Let it go."

And by then there were four more blazes.

The old man was really prepared.

"Are you trying to burn this place down?" Ash asked.

"I may unless you do something about those," Robert answered with a serene smile and a nod at some of the new fires.

Ash again did as he was told, but when he turned from it, he found half a dozen more infernos illuminating his yard, some of them large and much too near the house for his comfort.

"Damn it, Pap, what the hell are you doing?" he said as he rushed to where flames licked at the woodpile against the garage wall, while another crawled ever closer to the dry timber of the toolshed.

Robert stood in the midst of it all, looking satisfied with himself.

"We're going to have the fire department here any minute," Ash grumbled as he ran from throwing dirt onto a small fire to finally pull the hose out to spray the bigger ones.

But even though he was rushing around the yard and Robert had stopped lighting new blazes, there were so many burning already Ash couldn't keep them all under control himself.

"Don't just stand there," he told his grandfather. "This is getting out of hand and we're going to have real trouble here if you don't pitch in."

Robert stayed put. "You can do it all if you only work a little harder."

"Just put out that fire near the toolshed. The mower is in there and there's gas in it. The whole thing will explode."

"You can handle it. You're the only man for the job."

"Pap!" Ash shouted impatiently. "Put out that damn fire!"

"Are you sure about that?"

"Yes, I'm sure!"

Robert grinned broadly, then walked to his own yard next door and brought his hose over, joining in until together they had them all out.

Then he went down the garden path to the fire neither of them had touched and stood over it, staring at the few embers that were left of it.

"Okay, what's your point, old man?" Ash asked in a much calmer voice when he joined him.

But Robert only laughed, clapped him hard on the back, turned and walked away across the yards to disappear into his own house.

Alone in the night with the smell of smoke all around him, Ash glanced at his grandfather's handiwork and rubbed the sweat from his brow with the back of his arm. Then his gaze settled on the scant orange glow of the last few unattended embers smoldering at his feet on the garden path.

He stared down into those embers for a while, thinking about what his grandfather had done. And said.

Then he looked past them, at the garden beyond.

And only in that moment did he realize he was standing in the exact spot he'd stood five years before.

Where he and Beth had been married.

Chapter Eleven

"She doesn't want to see you, Ash," Jackson said. "And right now I don't think she should be upset. The doctor said she needs to rest."

But Beth wasn't resting. She was standing at the top of the stairs, listening to her brother doing as she'd asked—barring Ash's entrance at the front door.

It was barely seven in the morning and she'd been awakened first by the doorbell and then by Jackson informing her Ash was outside—before he'd even answered it—so he'd know what she wanted him to do.

It was Ash's voice that came next, in an even but deadly serious tone. "The last time you and I faced off at this door, Jackson, I took a punch I didn't have coming. That means I owe you one. Now I'm going to see Beth. Even if I have to repay that punch to do it."

Jackson stood his ground, as Beth knew he would, but she couldn't be the cause of a physical fight between the two of them. With a full, disgusted sigh preceding it, she said, "It's okay, Jackson, I'll see him if I have to."

Her brother didn't budge from blocking the doorway except to turn his face to her as she started down the steps. "Are you sure?"

"Yes."

With an expression that relayed neither approval nor disapproval, Jackson headed for the kitchen, freeing the way for Ash to come in.

From the entryway, Ash watched her descend the steps, his expression almost dangerous, his black eyes faintly shadowed and bloodshot. He looked like a man who hadn't slept in a long time, which was no doubt the case since he'd driven from one side of the state to the other and back again in less than twenty-four hours, in spite of the fact that Beth had had Jackson tell him not to come at all.

And yet, even though he showed evidence of how bone weary, worried and, once again, unhappy with her he was, she still had the urge to cross the entrance to him, slide her arms around his waist, lay her head against his chest and feel him envelop her with the strength and security of his body to reassure her everything would be all right.

But she didn't do any of that, because during the previous night she'd done a lot of thinking. Thinking that hadn't been fogged by her blinding love for Ash, by the feelings that had reawakened since he'd followed her here. Thinking that hadn't been distracted by the pure power of his presence.

And what she'd finally decided was this: Her baby deserved a full-time father. A loving home where its needs would always come first. Anything less just wasn't enough.

And even though she was having to battle the power of Ash's presence at that moment, she refused to lose sight of the way she knew things had to be between them.

"Why'd you come back?" she asked flatly, letting her tone convey that she wished he hadn't.

Ash ignored both her question and her attitude. "How are you? How is the baby?"

"Everything is fine," she answered almost airily, as if she hadn't been out of her mind with fear through it all. "I thought Jackson explained that on the phone last night."

Something in what she said seemed to anger Ash, because he closed his eyes tight and pinched the bridge of his nose. She saw his jaw clench as if he were working to control his temper.

But Beth wasn't sure what there was in such a simple statement to make him mad.

Jackson had arrived at the medical facility just after she had the evening before and had begun trying to locate Ash. Ash had left word at the lodge's front desk that an emergency had called him back to the reservation. But her brother hadn't been able to reach him there and he had ended up leaving several messages on the answering machines at the foundation office and at Ash's house.

Apparently Ash hadn't been at either place until the middle of the night, because when he'd received the messages at home at one this morning, he'd called right away.

But by then Beth had made up her mind, and she hadn't wanted to risk talking to him, afraid she might have broken down or wavered in the decisions she'd made. So she'd pleaded fatigue and had Jackson fill him in, which her brother had done. Thoroughly.

So what was there for Ash to be angry over? They'd done everything they could to let him know what was going on and had accepted a middle-of-the-night phone call from him, during which he'd been told all there was to tell.

Including that there was absolutely no reason for him to come back to Elk Creek.

After a moment, he took a deep breath and opened his eyes to her again. "Tell me yourself what happened."

"I think you ought to go to the lodge and get some sleep. You look awful," she said, rather than answer him, because even talking about the events of the previous evening put knots in her stomach.

Again his jaw tightened. "Tell me what happened," he repeated.

His tone and expression said he wasn't going anywhere until she did, so she figured she might as well get it over with.

Sliding her hands into the pockets of her bathrobe, she leaned against the banister, wanting to appear nonchalant about the whole thing. "I fell on the way home from the lake yesterday morning. Not bad, just a little tumble. I didn't think I'd hurt anything, but I guess it was enough to tear the placenta away from the uterus slightly, and that caused some pain and then some spotting. The doctor is sure there was no real harm done, though. The spotting and cramping stopped, the baby's heartbeat is great and an ultrasound test showed it doing just fine, so I was sent home to rest by about eleven last night. I'll go back in a couple of days to check on things, but there doesn't seem to be any problem." And there wasn't a single note in her voice that betrayed those knots in her stomach she'd been trying to avoid.

"Then this didn't happen from making love?"

"No, it didn't," she answered in a hurry. She certainly didn't want to discuss *that* subject. Just his saying the words raised goose bumps along her arms and much too vivid memories of pleasures she'd never have again.

"If you're supposed to be resting, I don't want you standing here," he said then. "Should you be in bed?"

"No, I only need to take it easy."

He nodded toward the living room. "Then let's go in there and sit down."

"Now that you know what happened and that the baby is fine, why don't you go get some sleep yourself?" she tried again.

He merely pointed a long index finger in the direction of the living room and stared at her as if the intensity of his eyes alone could move her through space.

Maybe it could, because even though she sighed impatiently, she went and sat on one of the sofas. "What was the emergency on the reservation?" she asked along the way.

Ash explained the crisis at the rehab center, but Beth paid only scant attention to what he was saying as she reminded herself that it had been a good thing he was called away. It had hammered home to her that in spite of the time they'd spent together in Elk Creek, in spite of the feelings he could raise in her, nothing had changed.

"If I'd have known everything wasn't all right with you and the baby, I wouldn't have gone. But as it was, I thought a little time for us both to cool off and think over the idea of our getting married again would be a good thing," he added when he'd finished.

Beth glanced at him where he stood not far away and wondered idly if even the threat of a miscarriage would have really kept him from the call of duty.

She knew he wasn't that unfeeling; he would have stayed with her at the doctor's—or at the hospital, if she'd needed to go.

But what about once the doctor had sent her home? When the worst of her jitters hit? When the adrenaline that came with fear finally waned and the full impact of what might have happened left her quivering in her bed?

After five years of experience she knew the answer to that. She knew that he would have been itching to get to the other crisis. And she knew she would have pretended everything was fine, that there was no reason for him to stay.

And that he'd have gone.

"I wish you would have thought to call Miss Lightfeather at home so she could have told you where I was or gotten hold of me herself sooner," he said then.

"It wouldn't have mattered," she lied. "There was nothing you could have done."

He let out a derisive, mirthless breath. "And you didn't need me or want me here, is that it?"

She raised her chin as if confirming it, all the while inside she was reliving just how much she *had* wanted and needed him. Too much. *Think of the baby,* she coached herself. *What kind of father do you want him to have?* "It was no big deal. I did okay on my own."

Ash sat on the coffee table in front of her and captured her eyes with his. "I don't believe that," he told her flat out and sternly. "I don't believe that you weren't scared to death that you'd lose this baby. I don't believe you didn't care that you were alone to face it. I don't believe that you didn't want me to be with you. What I can't handle is that you seem to think it's so damn bad to let me know it."

"It wouldn't have changed the fact that you were hundreds of miles away at the time," she pointed out. It would only have shown she was vulnerable and pitiable for having needs that wouldn't be met.

"No, it wouldn't have changed the fact that I was gone," he admitted. And with that, some of the steam seemed to go out of him, surprising her. "I'm sorry, Beth," he said then, taking her hands in his.

"Sorry for what?" she asked in a squeak of a voice as she worked to block the sparks that skittered up her arms at his touch.

"I'm sorry I wasn't here for you yesterday. I'm sorry I wasn't there for you through our whole marriage. I'm sorry I didn't see just how much I really did neglect you." He laughed a little wryly this time. "When I got home last night—before I saw the light on the answering machine and discovered Jackson's message—my grandfather was waiting for me, to point out a few things."

"Like what?"

"Like the fact that no matter how hard I work, I can't put out all the fires myself. And that I'm not the only one who can try. And that the price I paid for thinking I was, was losing you."

Beth didn't know what to say to that, so she didn't say anything at all. She just waited and watched him. And went on pushing hard against the wall that dammed her feelings for him behind it.

"I know I said before that I'd do what I could to cut back on work if you'd marry me again. And I know you didn't believe it could be done. But it can be, if I hire some help and delegate some of the work and responsibility."

"That costs money that's more needed other places," she parroted what she'd heard him say himself over the years, and then added the other reasons he'd always used against it. "And no one else carries the kind of clout or has the kind of connections you do after all your years of experience, or the drawing power to drum up funds and support. Plus, when you leave things to other people, they either get fouled up or at the very least are not done as efficiently or thoroughly or as well as when you do them yourself."

"Don't stab me with my own sword, Beth," he said, and she saw him waver in his belief that he could, indeed, successfully share the load. "I'm not saying it won't take time to find good people and teach them the ropes and introduce them around and build confidence in them. Or that I'm handing over the helm. What I'm saying is that if I hire some help, I can put this job more into the perspective it should be, and actually have a life with you and the baby."

Beth stared at him, loving him so much it hurt, memorizing every sharp plane of his handsome face and wanting to smooth away the lines that creased it with fatigue and stress. She knew he meant well. She knew he even believed that if he tried hard enough, he could do what he was proposing. And she believed he'd truly try.

But she knew him, knew how much he cared about his people and their plights, how responsible he felt, how duty bound to help, to make a difference. Those weren't the kinds of things that were just delegated, even to competent, capable people.

Beth shook her head and fought tears that threatened at the thought that no matter what he promised or how hard he tried, she and the baby still wouldn't be his first priority. They'd just be what kept him from doing what he felt he should. And she couldn't live that way. "It wouldn't work," she said very softly. "I know you want it to. I know you'd try to make it. But I also know that it won't. It can't.''

"It can with the right people," he insisted. "And if you meet me halfway and let me know if I'm getting too caught up in work and neglecting you or the baby, if you just speak up—" But he curbed the criticism and tried a different tack. "What about the time I've spent here? I've had Miss Lightfeather and my grandfather taking care of things, and until a major crisis came up, you and I were doing pretty well, weren't we? In fact, I was around more than you wanted me to be."

Again she shook her head, this time more vigorously. "But you were *here,* Ash, not in the thick of it. You and I both know that it's different being on the reservation, different when you haven't just temporarily postponed things to be away for a little while. And when you're right there, in the hub of what you care so much about, you are not going to be able to close your eyes to what needs attention. Or if you do you won't feel good about it, because I've whimpered or whined or nagged you into keeping your distance. And I won't feel good about it, either," she added quietly.

"Why is it that you always describe letting me know what you're feeling in such derogatory terms?" he shot out, clearly frustrated.

"I'm just calling it the way I see it. Besides, that's what it would sound like. And I couldn't do it any more than you could allow anyone else to put out one of those fires you knew was burning."

"Well, we could sure as hell give it a try, Beth."

He was angry again.

But then so was she, for his wanting to force her back into the same position that had made her leave him. "It just wouldn't work," she said again.

"Let's just try," he suggested as if soothing a skittish colt, squeezing her hands at the same time. "Come back to the reservation with me. We don't even have to get married right away if you want to wait until I've proven to you that we can work through it all, that I can cut back. And maybe once we have more time together like we have while I've been here, you'll see it isn't so tough to open up to me, too."

But as tempting as it was, she still shook her head against it, maintaining her denial. "I just don't believe either of us could pull it off. Old habits die hard—I've heard you say that a million times over the years. And no matter how honorable your intentions, I know you'll be drawn back into it all. And even if I could live with it, it isn't fair to the baby. The baby deserves more than that. It deserves a father who's there for it."

Too vivid in her mind was the memory of the past night, of letting herself think he would arrive any minute when the truth was he was gone, that in spite of his claims that he wanted to be a part of her pregnancy, a part of everything that was going on with her and the baby, he'd left at the drop of a hat.

Much as she loved him, she couldn't risk it happening again.

"I don't understand," he said harshly. "Are you saying it's better for the baby if its parents aren't together?"

"In this case, I'm afraid that's so. Not the way we'd be together." Beth willed herself to keep from crying.

"And that's it? Your final answer? To hell with me. To hell with your own feelings for me. To hell with being a family."

His words made her shudder internally. But all she could say was, "For the baby's sake, if not my own, I just don't think I have a choice."

This time it was Ash who shook his head. Clearly disgusted. Frustrated. So furious his jaw clenched once more.

But he didn't say anything. It was as if he couldn't trust himself to.

Instead, he stood and walked out, slamming the front door hard.

And the sound of that slamming door toppled the bricks of the dam that held her feelings contained, and they all suddenly came flooding out to drown her.

Chapter Twelve

"Are you all right?" Jackson asked Beth as he came out of the kitchen a moment later.

Beth didn't know her brother hadn't left the house after letting Ash in, and the realization that he was about to witness her falling apart jolted her back into control. She sat up straighter, squared her shoulders and blinked away the tears so perilously close to the surface.

"Sure. I'm fine," she managed.

But Jackson didn't seem convinced. He perched on the arm of the sofa, hooked a boot on the edge of the coffee table and frowned at her. "Shag would have been proud of you," he said, though it didn't sound like a good thing.

"You were listening?" But of course he had been, she thought. It was just like Jackson to be on the alert in case she'd needed him.

But all he said was "Voices carry."

Once more she found herself under a man's steady, unrelenting stare. And she was getting tired of it. "You look like you're busting to say something, Jackson. If that's the case, spit it out," she said peevishly.

That was all the invitation he seemed to need. "I don't mind tellin' you, Beth, I was worried that Ash wasn't doing right by you. But the truth is, it's you who's doing wrong. By Ash. By the baby. By yourself."

"Overhearing one conversation doesn't give you a complete picture."

"Gives me enough of it. Don't forget, I was raised by the same man, in the same way you were."

"That doesn't have anything to do with this."

"Maybe," Jackson allowed. "Then again, maybe it does."

Beth frowned back at him, wishing he'd leave her alone with her misery.

No such luck.

Jackson went on in that slow drawl of his. "Listening to Ash's side, it seems to me that Shag taught you too well to keep things to yourself."

Beth rolled her eyes at that, but began to be grateful for the rising anger that helped block the pain of having made what she believed to be the right decision against marrying Ash. Somehow it hurt even more than her earlier decision to divorce him. "Don't tell me you're advising me to turn into some simpering fool."

"Me?" he asked, shocked. "I'm the last one who'd do that. I'm just sayin' that when keeping your feelings to yourself means it costs you what you want most, it can't be all good."

She looked away from him and said flatly, "What makes you think I want Ash?"

Jackson blew out a derisive breath. "I was with you last night, remember? I was the one you kept sending to call him every five minutes. To find out anything I could about where he'd gone, if he'd be back, how to get hold of him. I was the one who watched you wishin' he was there so much you were nearly comin' apart at the seams. Now I hear you telling him to get lost for the baby's sake. But you and I know that's not what it's really about."

"It's all more complicated than you think, Jackson."

"Sounded pretty simple to me. Ash finally sees that he worked too much and is willing to hire some help so he can fix that. You're not willing to give him another chance because you're terrified of what it will do to you if he fails."

"That's an oversimplification." But was it?

Jackson ignored the comment. "Seems to me old Shag would have whupped the tar out of you for sitting back like some martyr and just being the silent, long-suffering wife. *Speak up for yourself* is what he'd have said."

Jackson sounded so much like their father when he mimicked him that it made her smile in spite of herself.

But he wasn't finished saying his piece. "Hell, Beth, even old Shag gave in to feelings for the opposite sex. You know he had a soft spot for Momma, and then there was Margie Wilson over at the café. And what about his lady friend in Denver those last years? He even left a full quarter share of everything to her, he must have loved her. You didn't see him counting it as a weakness and fighting against it the way you are."

Beth didn't have a comeback for that because it was true. It just hadn't ever occurred to her before.

Jackson stood then, apparently drawing his lecture to a close. "You have a baby to think of now," he said firmly. "And a whole life of your own stretchin' out ahead of you. You may think you're doing this for the child's sake, but are you? Have you considered that a second marriage *could* work? Have you considered the fact that Ash *could* change, that you might be depriving your child of a damn fine daddy after all?" He finished with a clear note of challenge in his voice, leaving her to think about it.

And she did think about it, because her brother's last comment rang in her ears.

Was she refusing to believe Ash could change because she was worried how she could bear it if he let her down again? Was she afraid of expressing her feelings to him and still coming up empty-handed?

But what had been accomplished by hiding them? she asked herself suddenly.

Sure, as a kid it had kept her from her father's wrath and harsh punishments. But as an adult it had cost her her marriage. It had caused her to walk from the lake so Ash wouldn't see her heart break and that had caused the fall that had put the baby in jeopardy.

Lord. She'd never thought of it like that before. But there it was now, frightening her to realize just how high a price she'd paid, how much more she could have paid.

And what about Jackson's perception that she wasn't standing up for herself?

That made sense, too.

But recognizing it and doing something about it were two different things.

Could she do it? Could she voice her needs to get them met if she and the baby began to slip down Ash's list of priorities? What if they got back to the reservation and being there, in the thick of the foundation's works and the problems that went with them, pulled him back in just as thoroughly as he'd been before? Would she really be able to pull him out again with complaints that would always ring in her ears as things she shouldn't be saying?

She didn't know.

And yet, when she really thought about what Ash had promised, she also realized that she should consider the kind of man she knew him to be. A man of intense pride and honor. A man who always kept his word. And he'd given her his word that he would do all he could to be a better husband. In fact, he'd given his word again and again that he'd try. If only she would...

Sitting there on that couch where Ash had left her, Beth had never felt so desolate.

She was facing the rest of her pregnancy and the birth of their baby alone—the way she'd been the night before.

She was facing raising the baby on her own.

But worst of all, she was facing the rest of her life without Ash. Without his love. Without his touch. Without sharing their child.

What she wanted, what she needed, was Ash as her husband. And as an active, full-time father to their baby. And there was only one chance of having that—if she met him halfway. No matter how tough that might be for her.

"Jackson!" she shouted in the direction of the kitchen, hoping her brother hadn't left the house.

Because she wasn't supposed to drive just yet.

And she needed to get to Ash before he really did give up on her.

* * *

One advantage to living in a small town was that Beth had no trouble getting a key to Ash's cabin at the lodge once she'd showered, dressed and fixed her hair and Jackson had driven her there.

She expected Ash to be asleep by then, so after assuring her brother he could go, she slipped quietly into the small, rustic room.

Ash was in bed, on his back, one arm across his eyes, the other over his bare chest, a sheet covering his lower half.

He'd taken a shower himself before he'd gone to bed. Beth knew because there was a faint lingering of steam from the bathroom. The smell of his soap was strong in the air, and the towel he'd used to dry off was on the floor beside the bed.

She wanted to crawl in with him, curl up close to what she suspected was his completely naked body under that sheet, and content herself with lying with him while he slept. But she knew she'd disturb him, so she merely sat in one of the chairs at the table, intent on waiting until he woke up.

No matter how long that might be.

Just being able to look at him helped her feel that it wasn't too late for them. That she could rescind the rejections and mistrust and doubts she'd heaped on him recently and make everything all right again.

"What are you doing, Beth?" His deep voice came then as he lifted his arm enough to let her see that he'd been watching her from beneath it.

"I'm sorry if I woke you."

"I wasn't asleep yet. I was having trouble getting there. For some reason I seem to have a lot on my mind."

"Like why in the world you ever thought you wanted to remarry someone so worried about being a fool for love that she was just a plain fool?"

"Like how I was going to prove to you I meant what I said about putting work into line behind you so I could convince you to marry me again."

"And how were you going to do that?" she asked, her curiosity piqued.

"I'm moving to Elk Creek, for starters," he said without anything hypothetical in it.

That surprised her. "What do you mean?"

He sat up in bed, raising one knee under the sheet at the same time to brace an arm on. "I've been thinking about what you said earlier this morning, and you're right. As long as I'm in the thick of things on the reservation, I'll be drawn into everything in spite of the best intentions. But I can run things from here if I hire some help, and then I won't be tempted to rush to every little fire that starts. And when I do need to leave to take care of something, you'll have your family and Kansas and—"

"But you'd be leaving your grandfather, your home, your roots, your traditions."

"In my tribe," he said with a tired smile, "it's the custom for the man to join the wife's people when they marry. I may be a little late, but I'll be upholding tradition to move here."

"But Ash," she persisted, still as if this whole idea was just conjectural, "what about ceremonies, the community, being a part of your heritage—"

"I can still go back for special occasions and participate. Being here won't make me less an Indian. Just more of a husband." His expression sobered then and he pinned her with those black eyes of his. "Because that's what I want to be, Beth. So if you came here to run me out of town on a rail, you'd better know you're going to have some trouble." Which led them back to his unanswered question about her being there. "Is that why you sneaked in here—to try to get me to leave?"

"No, it isn't," she answered quietly.

He nodded his approval of that and made a sound that was part sigh, part laugh, as if that were the most he expected to hear from her in the way of an invitation to stay or a statement of her commitment. "Tell me you love me, Beth," he said, sounding as exhausted as he looked. "If you never do it again for as long as we live, tell me now. Tell me that's why you're here and that it's enough to work out our problems."

"I do love you," she obliged, finding it easier than when she'd said it before. "Jackson gave me a good talking-to and pointed out a few things to me, but that was the one thing I knew even without his help."

The more she said, the higher his eyebrows arched, as if he couldn't believe she was speaking so freely. "Jackson's a good man, but what did he say that I didn't?" he asked, as if testing to see if she really was going to open up to him.

"Among a lot of things, there was one that really struck home—that I was so busy hiding my feelings from you I was refusing myself what I really wanted. I was so afraid of being disappointed again that I was denying the possibility that things could be different."

"An excellent observation. So here you are," he said then, tossing the ball into her court again.

"So here I am."

"And what happens now?"

She took a deep breath, shoring up her strength. "I decided that I'd like to give marriage a second try after all. That I know you'll do your best to keep your promise about not being swallowed up by the foundation—especially if you move here—and that I'm willing to wrestle with whatever I have to to do my part."

She stood and went to sit on the edge of his bed, facing him. "Because I really do love you, Ash. More than you'll ever know. And I want us to be together when this baby is born and through all the good and bad that comes with raising it, and—"

He reached up and cupped her cheek in his big palm and she lost her train of thought as she melted into his touch.

"You know, I've been pretty dumb myself, missing out on all we had together by not putting you first," he said. "I don't plan on letting that happen again, so there shouldn't be a need for you to do much complaining about my not being around. But there can never be enough of this kind of talk."

"You want me falling all over you, is that what you're telling me?" she joked through her third flash of tears, though now they were from happiness and the swell of love for him that rose from her heart to her throat.

"Physically you can fall all over me anytime," he joked back, caressing her face. "But verbally? Just a little will do. Just a periodic *hey you, I'm glad you're my husband.*"

"Will you be?"

"Will I be glad or your husband?"

"Both."

"Is that a proposal?" he asked in mock surprise.

"I thought you had one coming since I've turned down so many of yours."

"Yes, I'll gladly marry you and be your husband, a real one this time. And the best father I know how to be."

He pulled her to him then, capturing her mouth with his in a long, slow, deep kiss.

"I love you, Beth," he said when he ended it.

"I love you, too." She looked into his tired eyes and smoothed a finger along the dark shadow beneath one of them. "But you'd better get some sleep." She kicked off her shoes and raised the sheet, trying not to notice just how naked he was, and slipped into bed with him.

"I suppose sleeping is all we can do?" he asked, sounding resigned.

"For a few days, until the doctor gives us the go-ahead again."

He wrapped her in his arms and they lay back together, Beth curved to his side, her head on his chest.

"Then I guess we'll have to plan our second wedding around when we can have our honeymoon—as long as it won't be too far-off," he said.

"And in the meantime," she added, snuggling in very close to his gloriously naked body, "we can make the best of resting."

Except, at that moment, the baby gave a kick hard enough even for Ash to feel against his side.

"Looks like we're the only two who need it," he said with a laugh. "My son is ready to play."

"Or your daughter," Beth amended.

Ash slipped his hand between them to just the spot where the baby seemed to be dancing a jig, and Beth watched as his eyes closed and his face relaxed into an expression of pure contentment.

He couldn't go to sleep any too soon, because the wonders he was working at her middle were making it difficult to follow doctor's orders.

But she managed to conquer her rising desires by reminding herself that they'd have their whole lives to satisfy and delight in them.

The divorce just hadn't worked out.

* * * * *

*Beth and Ash have their baby—
and Jackson Heller meets his match—
in Book Three of Victoria Pade's
A RANCHING FAMILY. Watch for*
Cowboy's Kiss, *available in July 1995—
only from Silhouette Special Edition!*

Get Ready to be Swept Away by
Silhouette's Spring Collection

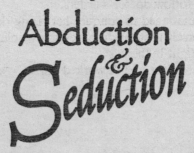

Abduction & Seduction

These passion-filled stories explore both the dangerous
desires of men and the seductive powers of women.
Written by three of our most celebrated authors, they are
sure to capture your hearts.

Diana Palmer
Brings us a spin-off of her Long, Tall Texans series

Joan Johnston
Crafts a beguiling Western romance

Rebecca Brandewyne
New York Times bestselling author
makes a smashing contemporary debut

Available in March at your favorite retail outlet.

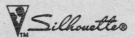

Silhouette celebrates motherhood in May with...

Debbie Macomber
Jill Marie Landis
Gina Ferris Wilkins

in

Three Mothers & a Cradle

Join three award-winning authors in this
beautiful collection you'll treasure forever.
The same antique, hand-crafted cradle
connects these three heartwarming romances,
which celebrate the joys and excitement of
motherhood. Makes the perfect gift for yourself
or a loved one!

A special celebration of love,

Only from ▼ *Silhouette*®
TM

—where passion lives.

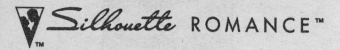

Silhouette ROMANCE™

Arriving in April from Silhouette Romance...

Bundles of Joy

Six bouncing babies. Six unforgettable love stories.

Join Silhouette Romance as we present these heartwarming tales
featuring the joy that only a baby can bring!

***THE DADDY PROJECT* by Suzanne Carey**
***THE COWBOY, THE BABY AND THE RUNAWAY BRIDE*
by Lindsay Longford**
***LULLABY AND GOODNIGHT* by Sandra Steffen**
***ADAM'S VOW* by Karen Rose Smith**
***BABIES INC.* by Pat Montana**
***HAZARDOUS HUSBAND* by Christine Scott**

Don't miss out on these BUNDLES OF JOY—only from Silhouette Romance.
Because sometimes, the smallest packages can lead to the biggest surprises!

And be sure to look for additional BUNDLES OF JOY
titles in the months to come.

BOJ1

the exciting new series by
New York Times bestselling author

The MacKade Brothers—looking for trouble,
and always finding it. Now they're on a collision
course with love. And it all begins with

**THE RETURN OF RAFE MACKADE
(Intimate Moments #631, April 1995)**

The whole town was buzzing. Rafe MacKade
was back in Antietam, and that meant only one
thing—there was bound to be trouble....

Be on the lookout for the next book in the
series, **THE PRIDE OF JARED MACKADE—
Silhouette Special Edition's 1000th Book!**
It's an extraspecial event not to be missed,
coming your way in December 1995!

THE MACKADE BROTHERS—these sexy, trouble-
loving men will be heading out to you in alter-
nate books from Silhouette Intimate Moments
and Silhouette Special Edition.
Watch out for them!

A ROSE AND A WEDDING VOW (SE #944)
by Andrea Edwards

Matt Michaelson returned home to face Liz—his brother's widow...a woman he'd never forgotten. Could falling in love with *this* Michaelson man heal the wounds of Liz's lonely past?

A ROSE AND A WEDDING VOW, SE #944 (3/95), is the next story in this stirring trilogy by Andrea Edwards. THIS TIME, FOREVER—sometimes a love is so strong, nothing can stand in its way, not even time. Look for the last installment, A SECRET AND A BRIDAL PLEDGE, in May 1995.